THEY CALL ME MIRANDA

THEY CALL ME MIRANDA

Sara Judge

CHIVERS
THORNDIKE

This Large Print edition is published by BBC Audiobooks Ltd, Bath, England and by Thorndike Press®, Waterville, Maine, USA.

Published in 2004 in the U.K. by arrangement with Robert Hale, Ltd.

Published in 2004 in the U.S. by arrangement with Robert Hale, Ltd.

U.K. Hardcover ISBN 0–7540–6962–1 (Chivers Large Print)
U.S. Softcover   ISBN 0–7862–6655–4 (Nightingale)

The text of this Large Print edition is unabridged.
Other aspects of the book may vary from the original edition.

Set in 16 pt. New Times Roman.

Printed in Great Britain on acid-free paper.

British Library Cataloguing in Publication Data available

Library of Congress Control Number: 2004104818

ONE

I am a very fortunate young woman. Mrs Beadle keeps telling me so, and she is a correct and God-fearing lady so it must be true. My husband, Mr Robert Hawton, is a tall man of pleasing countenance, and my little son, Charles Robert, gives me more pleasure with every passing day.

Yet deep inside worry and loneliness haunt me, for I am without memory, knowing neither my name nor my rightful age.

Mrs Beadle says it is foolish to be anxious; she says I should make the most of all that I have now, there is so much for which to be thankful, why worry about the past? Mr Hawton knows all about my past and if he does not see fit to explain my background to me, then leave well alone. Mrs Beadle has implicit faith in my husband, her eyes follow him devotedly whenever he is in the room with us, and she hangs upon his words as if he were some prophet of old.

Mr Hawton is gentle with me and very polite, yet there is an invisible wall between us through which I cannot reach him. And always the thought—he knows! But he will tell me nothing.

Why? What have I done? How did I come to lose my memory? And why should the truth be kept a secret? Surely I have a right to know?

But the few times I have attempted to question Mr Hawton he has been abrupt, almost angry, and I dare not keep pestering him for information.

'Allow me to be the best judge of such matters, Miranda,' he told me coldly the last time I asked for the truth. 'The facts you require are not necessary to your present way of life and would only cause you further mental anguish. Be satisfied with what you now possess; be thankful for recovered health, and your strong and beautiful son. I have given you a home, security and my affection. No female should expect more from life.'

I am grateful, yes, and happy for most of the time. But satisfied? Never. I shall never feel complete contentment until this blanket has lifted from my mind and I learn everything about myself and the years before I came to Hazelwood.

Tomorrow my new companion comes to stay. Mrs Beadle has to leave us, for her sister has become ill and she must go to nurse her. I shall not be sorry to see the back of her. She has been my constant companion since the earliest days, since our stay at the Ram Inn in Hertford, before my marriage. She is most efficient and clever at needlework; she knows at once when my head begins to ache, and is good about going up to see Charlie when I am poorly, and giving me news of him. But she is also stiff and humourless and elderly. So now Mr Hawton has decided on a younger woman, and when he takes Mrs Beadle into town he will return with Miss Betsy Potter.

How I long to see her! And to talk and laugh with somebody new and gay. My husband is often sunk in gloom, and Mrs Beadle has no sense of fun. I long to converse with someone nearer my own age and forget my problems in light-hearted chatter. Was I frivolous before? Impossible to know, but this dreary house does nothing to lift my spirits and I am too often depressed and irritable. All I know about Betsy is the fact that she comes from the vicarage on the outskirts of Aylesbury, and that the parson is a distant relative of Mr Hawton.

I shall remain in the care of Mrs Wanstead, the housekeeper, whilst my husband is away. It is a strange thing but I have never been left on my own since coming to Hazelwood, indeed, since as far back as my memory goes. Did I perhaps try to take my own life some time ago? That might account for the hideous scar which runs from my left eye-brow high up into my hair, and for the fact that Mr Hawton will never leave me unattended.

Mrs Wanstead is a dear motherly soul, very different from Mrs Beadle. I wish that she could have been my companion this last year, but she is a competent and thrifty housekeeper, so my husband tells me, for I know nothing of such matters, and ever busy with this large establishment.

We live very grandly at Hazelwood; there is a magnificent chandelier in the hall, which glistens like dripping diamonds when the candles are lit, and there are two more in the long drawing-room, and one above the dining-table.

There is a gallery around the hall and on the walls Mr Hawton's ancestors gaze down with supercilious stares from their gilt frames. We possess seven bedrooms, and Charlie has a set of rooms for himself and his nurse upstairs, and there is an extra chamber which will later be his schoolroom.

Oh, I am lucky, lucky! Many girls would envy me my life here and long to be mistress of such an elegant home. Yet always the same doubt lurks at the back of my mind, and before a migraine the anxiety is worse; who am I? Where do I come from? How did I come to make Mr Hawton's acquaintance?

*   *   *

At last the day has come and I have waved farewell to Mrs Beadle and now eagerly await Miss Betsy Potter's arrival.

Mrs Wanstead is sitting opposite me with her knitting, and she smiles as I keep moving to the long glass windows to peer out at the

4

drive. But the carriage has not yet returned, and the gravel lies golden and untrampled in the sunshine, whilst petunias bloom scarlet and pink and purple in their grey stone urns.

'Not yet, ma'am, you must be patient,' the housekeeper says behind me.

'But I want to see her—I long to know what she is like. Betsy is young, like me, and I am so looking forward to having her come and stay with us.'

I remain standing by the window, afraid to sit down in case I should miss her arrival. These windows face south; across the drive are sloping lawns bordered by huge bushes of rhododendrons and azaleas, and beyond them is park-land stretching to the distant road. Our drive winds for nearly a mile up to the house, and on either side are open spaces shaded here and there by massive oaks.

Behind the house is the vegetable garden and at the side are the stables, where Mr Hawton keeps his big bay hunter, and my lovely, dancing Cloud. She is a dapple-grey, and I was so proud when my husband presented her to me; for until last month all my lessons were upon staid Mary, a stout, placid creature on whom I spent many a weary hour. But I learned to ride, and ride well, by the time Old George, the head groom, finished with me. And I still go down to see Mary and stroke her soft nose, for she taught me not to fear the unaccustomed height and motion

5

from the top of a horse's back. On Cloud I am now allowed to canter across the park, but Old George always accompanies me. I am never allowed to go out riding alone.

Fortunately no one has suggested that I go hunting. I would certainly refuse, and dread the time when Charlie grows older and first takes his place in the field. It is a cruel and wicked sport, and my feelings are all for the fox. They may do harm, as Mr Hawton often tells me, explaining about the chickens and geese which are frequently stolen by the red marauders. But I have seen good land marred by countless hooves, and hedges and fences broken by the onslaught of horsemen, and wonder which causes more damage to the farmer—the hunted or the hunters?

Although I love horses I am not fond of dogs. Mr Hawton owns a huge brute, called Bella, and a bloodhound by breed. What a horrible name! She is gentle enough in temperament, and has formed an attachment for me which I find both embarrassing and irritating. Everything about her is loose and floppy—sagging jowl, red-rimmed eyes, hanging folds of brown skin; she repulses me but does not appear daunted by my obvious dislike. She does not even stay outside in a kennel, but Mr Hawton allows her to enter the house, and she sleeps on the rug in the library each night. Fortunately she does not go into any other rooms, and as she accompanies my husband wherever he goes I do not see much of her.

The library is Mr Hawton's domain, and Bella's, whilst I have a pretty sitting-room of my own on the other side of the hall. Only Charlie is allowed to visit me there, and when my husband and I are together in the evenings, we sit in the long drawing-room where I am now waiting with Mrs Wanstead.

There—they have arrived at last! I see my husband pulling up the horses and beside him, neat and demure in a grey suit, sits a small bonneted figure. Old George comes round to assist the lady down, he must always be the first to view a newcomer, and one of the under -grooms runs to hold the horses' heads as Mr Hawton carelessly flings aside the reins and jumps down at the far side of the carriage. Then round he comes to escort Miss Potter into the house, and I move forward into the hall to greet my new companion.

*   *   *

'You look lovely, ma'am,' says Betsy, standing back to admire her handiwork. We are upstairs and my new friend is helping me to dress for the evening. 'With those little curls pulled forward the scar is scarcely noticeable, and there is something most attractive about such short curls.'

'Oh, Betsy, do you think so?' My hair is my

7

abomination, but at least it looks like hair now and not the ugly stubble which I had to keep covered with a scarf, wrapped turban-like around my head for so many months. It had to be kept cropped, close to my head, because of the foul-smelling ointment which Mrs Beadle rubbed into my scalp both night and morning.

'It will help the scar to fade, dear,' she always insisted. 'You don't want to have that unsightly blemish all your days, now, do you?'

I did not. But began to feel that even the purplish wound would be preferable to the stickiness and odour of Dr Ingram's cream. However, a month ago the doctor gave in to my pleading and I am now allowed to grow my hair, and have thrown the last of his vile ointment away.

So the curls are growing; silky-soft and almost black in colour, they spring up all over my head in wayward abandon. Mrs Beadle did not like them at all and tried to grease them down, but this new style suits me and softens my face. I do not look in the least like the smooth-headed ladies whom I have seen in periodicals, with heavy chignons or sleek ringlets on either side of their cheeks.

'There is nothing so becoming as hair worn smooth upon the brow to show off one's features.' Betsy pats her own neat head with complacent fingers. 'But you have a style of your own, ma'am, and you must tell me if Mr Hawton remarks upon your appearance this evening.'

'Oh, but I think he would wish you to be present, Betsy. I am sure that he expects you to dine with us.'

Mrs Beadle did not take her meals with us, preferring the cosy intimacy of Mrs Wanstead's parlour. But Betsy Potter is a distant kinswoman of my husband, and will thus be welcome to sit at our table.

It will also help me if she is present. Sometimes I find it hard to converse through the meal and if Mr Hawton is in a silent mood, sunk in dark thought as he so often is, it will relieve the atmosphere to have this young girl sitting with us.

'What beautiful jewels, ma'am,' Betsy sighs, as she fastens diamond and sapphire earrings in my ears.

I can see her standing behind me, her eyes sparkling in the candle-light, making her appear almost pretty. She is a small, neat person, dowdily dressed in grey serge, and with red, work-worn hands which feel harsh as they brush against my skin. Her hair is a dull brown, pulled back tightly into a knot behind her little head, and her eyes are strangely colourless—a very light grey, like water. But when she is animated her pale face glows and the odd-coloured eyes have an unusual attraction.

'We must see about new clothes for you, Betsy,' I say, standing up and comparing my deep-blue taffeta to her rough cloth. Later, for

Christmas, perhaps, or for her birthday, I shall give her a brooch or a ring. Beautiful objects obviously please her and I have so much, it will be a joy to bestow some of my many possessions upon her.

'There is a competent seamstress in the village whom I shall ask to come up and make some new dresses for you. Brown or grey will do very well for the day-time, but I insist on you wearing more attractive colours and fabrics in the evenings.'

'Oh, ma'am,' she breathes, clapping her hands together, 'will I really have new clothes to wear? I cannot believe it! This gown belonged to Mercy Rushmore, and my Sunday best is also a hand-me-down. I cannot remember ever wearing a new dress.'

'Then you shall at Hazelwood.' I smile down at her for she is several inches smaller than I am. 'I am going up to the nursery now to say goodnight to my son, then I shall be in the drawing-room with Mr Hawton. Change into your Sunday best for this evening and then come down and join us.'

My husband likes to see me in a different gown at night, and I wear the jewels he gives me, for otherwise they would lie forgotten in a drawer. We never entertain, except for the occasional visits from the parson, nor do we dine out at other houses.

At first this isolation did not trouble me; I was still recovering from my illness when I married Mr Hawton, and then with Charlie on the way invitations would have been impossible. The birth of my son was an unpleasant and painful affair and it is only now, nine months after his arrival, that I begin to feel really well. Head-aches still occur, but Dr Ingram assures me that these bouts will cease in time, and he has given me excellent powders which relieve most of the pain.

I enjoy riding, and Charlie gives me increasing pleasure as he grows older, but otherwise my life is lonely so I was overjoyed when Mr Hawton announced that Miss Potter was coming to stay.

Charlie's rooms are on the floor above, next to the linen room and the maids' bedrooms, and he lives there under the tender care of Helen Morris.

Fortunately for us all, Helen was free to come the moment Charlie was born, for I was far too weak to suckle him, and she had recently lost her own child and had a plentiful supply of milk. She was not married, poor girl, and though I was shocked at first to hear this, Helen soon put my mind at rest for she is devoted to my son.

I take him now and hold his warm, firm little body close against me. He puts out a chubby fist, fascinated by the gems in my ears, and then buffets my head as I pull laughingly away from him.

'Gently, dearie, not so hard,' says Helen

anxiously, moving forward to catch his hand in hers. 'You must not hurt your Mama—gently now.'

'It's all right, Helen, he doesn't hurt me.' I plant a kiss upon his fat cheek and he chortles and pats my face, his hand soft and moist against my skin. Charlie has very fair hair and large grey-blue eyes, and is quite beautiful.

'We have a new lady in the household,' I tell the girl, moving to the rocking chair and setting Charlie upon my lap. 'She is to take Mrs Beadle's place and her name is Miss Betsy Potter.'

'Yes, ma'am.' Helen's bright eyes survey me with interest. She is a red-haired, freckle-faced girl, with a sturdy, peasant's figure and a sunny smile. I know very well that she will have heard the news from the other servants, but it gives me something to say. I find it so hard to converse, have difficulty talking to my husband, am uneasy with Helen and the maids. Even with Mrs Beadle I was often tongue-tied, but she chattered so much that my silence passed unnoticed. Perhaps now, with Betsy, I shall be able to lose my reticence and partake in normal conversation. But it is uncommonly hard to talk when one knows so little about oneself. Have I a family? Are there brothers and sisters waiting for me to come home? Is a mother weeping at nights for her lost daughter? I have no memories—no past— how can I begin to talk like an ordinary human being?

Stiffly I rise and hand Charlie back to his nurse, my brow contracting with bitter thoughts. My head is beginning to throb. Why will my husband not tell me about my past life? It is cruel behaviour which is incomprehensible to me.

'Thank you, Helen, he is looking well. I shall be in to see him again tomorrow. Good-night, my darling.' I bend to kiss Charlie's downy head as he nestles drowsily against the girl's shoulder. 'Sweet dreams. Mama will see you in the morning.'

I leave the room and go downstairs to join my husband hoping that Betsy will soon come and save me from another evening of forced politeness over the dinner-plates.

That night, after Betsy has helped me into my nightgown and tidied away my clothing, she brushes my hair carefully for my scalp is still tender where the scar has formed. Then she slips away to her own room further down the passage, and I lie and wait for Mr Hawton.

He visits me every night before retiring himself, and I dread his presence in my bedchamber. I cannot see the sense of these nocturnal visits, for we have already spent the evening together and exhausted all our trivial conversation. But always he comes, before withdrawing to his own bedroom which adjoins mine.

'Do you think that you will be happy with

13

Betsy?' he asks, sitting stiffly on the end of my bed, his face in profile.

'Very happy. She seems a friendly and intelligent girl and I am sure we will get on well together.'

Betsy had joined us for our evening meal, but presumably Mr Hawton's presence overawed her, for she contributed nothing towards our talk and sat demurely, eyes downcast, for the entire meal.

'She has youth on her side, also,' my husband now remarks, 'and will be able to walk and ride with you, which Mrs Beadle was not able to do.'

He stares down at the carpet and I notice how arrogantly his nose juts from his face, how thickly his dark hair curls as it touches his collar. His brows are well-marked but his mouth is too severe, he seldom smiles and I have never heard him laugh.

Why did Mr Hawton choose me as his life's companion? No one can say that we are happy in each other's company; he is a handsome man who could no doubt have taken his pick from any number of young girls to be his bride. Why me? I am unattractive with my scarred face and boyish hair, too tall, and also dull and burdensome with my lack of knowledge and frequent headaches. Whilst my husband is a mature gentleman, certainly a good few years older than I am, and he must meet many beautiful and accomplished ladies in town, for he is often away in London staying at his club.

'Why do you not take me with you to London?' I voice my thoughts, determined to try and make him give me information. 'Are you ashamed of me?'

He smiles and looks directly at me. 'Not ashamed, only conscious of your frailty. I would not have you tired by the journey, and the doctor says you are not strong enough for parties and entertaining.'

'But you will take me one day?'

'Perhaps.' He stands and moves forward to kiss my forehead. 'You are not unhappy here, Miranda? You must tell me if there is anything you want. You are pleased with the new mare, are you not?'

'Cloud? Oh, yes, I love her. And indeed I have every comfort, thank you, sir. But I want to know about myself. How can I be a complete person with this blanket across my mind?' I look up at him pleadingly, but he turns abruptly and walks to the door.

'I have told you before—do not question me. It is best that you know nothing about your past. Trust me, Miranda.' He looks back at me, his hand upon the door knob. 'Your well-being is important to me, I do assure you, and beg that you concentrate fully on the present and build a future here at Hazelwood. The future is what matters—for you and Charlie and myself. The past is finished and done with, try to subdue all curiosity and live

15

for now, for the present, and for this family.'

Mr Hawton leaves me alone and I snuff out the candle beside me, feeling dissatisfied and more puzzled than ever.

Next morning Betsy and I retire to my sitting-room after breakfast. It is a bright, sunny room overlooking the rose garden, and a fire is lit here first thing in the morning during the winter and spring. I keep my sewing here and have my own collection of books. They come from the nursery, and are all volumes which Mr Hawton and his brother possessed when they were young. I do not think that I was badly educated, for I have found both French and Latin text books on the shelves upstairs, and am able to understand them; yet I have no knowledge of the more commonplace children's books, and am now making up for lost time.

I always have flowers in my little sanctuary, and take great pleasure in arranging the blooms which Mrs Wanstead leaves on the marble-topped table in the hall, every morning.

There are a couple of pretty water-colour paintings on the walls, which Mr Hawton allowed me to bring in here to make the room more homely. I do not care for most of the pictures in this house, for they are in oils and depict sombre ladies and gentlemen, or else hunting scenes.

'What a charming room,' says Betsy, as we

make ourselves comfortable.

My husband has gone about his business for the day, riding out with his steward to see how the new drainage system is progressing, and I sit at my tapestry whilst Betsy prepares to read to me. She has chosen Robinson Crusoe, and her voice is clear but a little sharp in tone, and I am glad when she reaches the end of the first chapter.

'Tell me about yourself,' I say, as she draws breath. 'Do you have any brothers or sisters? Is this your first position?'

She folds her hands upon the book and settles back in her chair.

'I am an only child, ma'am, but was brought up with the parson's brood—five boys and girls, he has, and they are like family to me.'

'Then you are not the clergyman's daughter?' I stare across at her. 'I understood from my husband that you were a distant relative of his?'

'Oh, no, ma'am!' She laughs, showing tiny white teeth, like a kitten's. 'Parson Rushmore is some sort of cousin of Mr Hawton's, I believe, but I am a farmer's daughter. Father died some years back and we were so poor that Parson Rushmore kindly took us in. He had lately lost his wife, so Mother keeps house for him and I was educated with his own children. Reading and writing and sums—even a bit of Latin.' She nods sagely. 'I am passably well educated for a girl.'

17

'You are, indeed. And what are the names of the other children—how old are they?'

Being without family myself, details of other people's lives are vastly interesting. Mrs Beadle was a childless widow, with but the one ailing sister, and my husband's only brother is dead. Between us we have Charlie, that is all.

Betsy begins counting on her fingers. 'There's Solomon and Adam, the two eldest boys, then Mercy, who is my age, and the two younger ones are Charity and little Hope.'

I smile. 'Those names are just right for a parsonage.'

'But your name, ma'am, if I may be so bold.' She leans forward. 'I have not heard it before except in Shakespeare. Were you named after the heroine in The Tempest?'

'Did Mr Hawton not tell you?' My voice is cold. 'I have lost my memory and they call me that because everyone must have a name.' I lower my head and concentrate upon my needlework.

'Yes, your husband said that you could not remember things and had been very sick a while back,' says Betsy softly, 'but I did not realise that you didn't know your own name. How far back can you remember? Is there a beginning, so to speak, in your mind? Do you mind me asking such questions, ma'am, only it is ever so romantic, really.'

'Romantic?' I have not considered my affliction in such a way before.

'Yes. You might be a princess, or a titled lady, or famous. Oh, all sorts of exciting notions come to mind! How I wish we could find out the truth!' Her eyes are sparkling again as she sits forward. 'I suppose it all happened on account of that scar?'

'It was a heavy blow, so the doctor says, but it could not have been under pleasant circumstances else Mr Hawton would have told me about it.'

'He knows?' Betsy stares in astonishment. 'Mr Hawton knows all about you? Then why does he not speak?'

'Of course he knows,' I say sharply, 'how else could he have known me well enough to marry?'

'I thought perhaps that he met you in London, after you had lost your memory, and married you without knowing anything of your background. What did your last companion say? For how long have you been like this?'

'Mrs Beadle knew nothing but implied that I was a most fortunate young lady and should put my trust in my husband. She admired him greatly, which is understandable, but I cannot help feeling dissatisfied, Betsy.' I lay down my sewing in vexation. 'It is my life, you see, not theirs, and thus of infinite importance to *me*. Yet no one seems to care about how I feel inside. Material comforts abound—I have fine clothes, warmth, good food and a grand house. Oh, yes, I have much to be grateful for. But

19

there is such mental torment at times which nothing can appease. Who am I, Betsy? Where do I come from? Can you see the frustrating situation in which I am placed?'

'Of course, ma'am, I understand. But you must not excite yourself. Mr Hawton said that you were to be kept calm and not allowed to become agitated or distressed.' She springs up and tugs at the velvet rope beside the mantel. 'I shall ask for tea and biscuits to be brought to us—a nice hot cup of tea will steady you and bring comfort.'

'I am quite controlled, thank you, Betsy.'

The days of panic are over, those days when I used to waken from turbulent nightmares, from dreams filled with wild thoughts and unnamed horrors; mornings when Mrs Beadle had to give me powders with my first drink of the day and sit beside me, stroking my brow until I fell back into oblivion once again. They had been fearful, those first weeks of consciousness, and so jumbled were my thoughts that it is difficult to remember now what was fact and what fiction.

'I can remember staying at the Ram Inn in Hertford,' I say slowly, taking my mind as far back as I can. 'That would have been before I married Mr Hawton. He came to visit us and took us out driving, and I can remember the little church and my wedding-day.'

Misty, dream-like sequences pass across my brain; Mrs Beadle, severe and gaunt-faced in

20

her plumed bonnet and plaid shawl, for it had been a winter's day, with a biting east wind. And Mr Hawton, tall and serious beside me, holding my hand tightly as I slipped it from my muff. And velvet, cream-coloured velvet for me, with a floor-length cloak of the same material, and a hood trimmed with fur. There were no flowers, as far as I can remember, and no guests. Only Mrs Beadle and a small fat man to witness our marriage. Strange ceremony, strange bride! I sigh and lift my handiwork to resume sewing.

'My first clear memories are of this house and walking in the grounds with Mrs Beadle. For a long time before that I was still sick, you see, and everything is so dim and muddled. Then there was Charlie, and learning to ride. All these are what I have now, they are the present and—and right.' I give myself a little shake. 'It is important to concentrate on the present—my past is over and done with—let it lie.'

'For the moment,' says Betsy, 'for the moment we will leave things as they are. I must get to know this house and meet your son, and then we will go out together and walk over the estate. Do not forget that I am a farmer's daughter and thus interested in the land. And we will talk and get to know each other better. Then later, maybe, you will begin to remember more.'

'If that were only possible!'

21

'What does the doctor say? Mr Hawton told me that he visits once a month.'

'Poor Dr Ingram. He comes and feels my pulse and nods his head and makes encouraging noises in his throat.' I smile. 'But he is as perplexed as I am, poor man.'

'But has he not said that your memory will return one day?'

'It is possible but improbable. This blow I received,' my hand goes up to finger the hateful scar, 'this blow was heavy and he says I was fortunate not to have lost my sight, or even my life. But nobody knows what caused the accident—except my husband—and he is not telling.'

One of the maids brings in the tea-tray then and we are silent for a moment.

'Thank you, Rose.'

She bobs a curtsey and goes out closing the door behind her.

'You cannot come from this part of the country,' says Betsy, leaning forward to pour out the tea. 'Or somebody would have recognised you by now.'

'Recognised me, how so? I never go out, except to church, and the congregation is only made up of people from the village. I have not even been back to Hertford since my wedding-day. I don't suppose anybody knows that I am here—it is almost as if Mr Hawton is hiding me away from the world.'

'Has he no family, no relations? Does

nobody ever visit?'

I shake my head. 'The doctor comes, and the parson, on occasion, when he wants more money. No one else has been to the house since I have lived here.'

'It is wondrous strange,' murmurs Betsy, handing me a cup of tea.

There are macaroons, and buttered scones, and Cook's special oat cakes, all set out on the Royal Doulton plates. It is surprising that I have not put on weight since living at Hazelwood, but my waist is still laced to twenty inches, and my wrists and ankles remain slender.

'I shall have to walk a great deal,' remarks Betsy, as if in answer to my thoughts. 'I do so love the food you have here, and am already over plump.'

Her honesty amuses me.

'No such thing! You have a trim little figure and are exactly right as you are. Do you ride, Betsy? It is my favourite form of exercise.'

Her eyes widen in alarm. 'Oh, no, ma'am, I've never been on a horse in my life and have no desire to, either.'

'But a farmer's daughter? Surely you must have ridden as a child?'

'Riding is for the gentry.' Betsy's eyes harden and her lips go tight. 'How could Father have found money for a horse when we had scarcely enough for the cows and pigs which were our livelihood? No, ma'am, horse-riding was not for the likes of me—I was brought up to work, not go gallivanting about the countryside jumping ditches and ruining good crops!'

'Aha! Just as I thought. Some farmers are not fond of the hunt, then?'

Betsy continues to look grim so I explain hastily about Mary.

'I learned to ride on her and she is so gentle you will feel quite safe. Do please try, Betsy, I want to show you the estate, and the fields can only be properly explored on horseback. But we will be very careful where there are crops,' I add.

'If you insist, ma'am,' she mutters, 'but I cannot say I relish the idea.'

TWO

That afternoon we go down to the stables, Betsy and I, and she is introduced to Old George and Mary. Cloud comes forward in her box, nuzzling at my arm for the sugar she loves, and laughingly I give her what she craves. And Betsy must stroke her nose and admire her, although I can see that she would rather stand back and look from a distance.

'Very nice,' she says, retreating, as Cloud blows down her velvety nostrils at the visitor. 'Very nice, I'm sure, but I do wish horses were smaller animals. And such big feet!' She stares in alarm as Old George leads Cloud out into the yard.

'I won't be riding today,' I say regretfully, watching the mare's slender, impatient legs and the ripple of muscles beneath her satiny coat. 'Let one of the lads give her a good gallop, George, she needs to be ridden daily but I shall be showing Miss Potter the gardens this afternoon.'

Old George touches his cap as we move away, and Betsy, relief in her voice, trips along beside me.

'I shall never dare, ma'am. Never shall I sit upon one of those beasts. Oh, why cannot we walk, ma'am, and explore the estate at our leisure on foot?'

Her fear gives me confidence and I am delighted all over again with my new companion.

'Nonsense, Betsy, dear. I felt just the same as you and shivered for minutes both before and after my first ride. But Old George will help you and so will dear solid Mary, who could not gallop to save her life!' I smile down at the girl, then take her hand and lead her round to the front of the house. 'Come, we shall walk in the gardens and you can forget your fright. Then, later, I shall take you up to meet Charlie.'

'Where is the village?' asks Betsy. 'We came through it yesterday but I am not too sure of my direction.'

I point. 'There—over beyond the trees— you can just see the church tower from here. You will meet Parson Andrews soon, no doubt. Mr Hawton often reads the lesson on Sundays, but I must confess that I find the services dreadfully boring.'

'That is a pity.' Betsy has turned pink. 'We always attended church twice on Sundays and once mid-week, as well. Are you not religious, ma'am?'

Her prim tone annoys me. 'How do I know? When you see the church and hear the parson perhaps you will understand. He talks over-long about nothing and is always asking Mr Hawton for more money.'

' 'Tis for the poor,' she replies swiftly, 'and it

is right that the squire should give to those less fortunate than himself. Do you not take food and clothing to the cottagers? Mercy and I often went round the village at home with gifts for the needy. Not that we had much ourselves, but we made blankets from old pieces of wool and cloth, and Mother always cooked extra soup when she could manage it. It is a charitable thing to do, and you have so much—why should you not help others?'

I stare at her. 'I never go into the village. They will all gawk at me like they do in church, and wonder about my scar and discuss me behind my back. Anyway, Mr Hawton would not like it.'

'It is your duty,' replies my companion fiercely. 'Most of the men must labour on this estate—what other work is there for them out here in the country? And on what they earn it must be difficult to stay alive, particularly if they have children.'

'What kind of talk is that? And how do you know so much?'

'Because I was born and bred on the land and Father was but a poor farmer, beholden to the squire for too many things. And we starved due to bad harvests and a selfish and uncaring landowner. Oh, I could tell you some tales, ma'am, memories of my childhood which are far from pleasant.' She shuts her lips firmly together and gazes ahead of her, striding out so quickly that I am forced into a run to keep up with her.

I am learning something new every time Betsy opens her mouth. But then my own worries have taken up all my attention until now, and certainly, neither Mrs Beadle nor Mrs Wanstead have ever spoken to me in such open fashion.

'Come, Betsy,' I say gently, 'let us think of happier things. Come and see the gardens.'

There will surely be no chance of controversy there, and the rose garden, with its old weathered sun-dial in the centre, is one of my favourite places.

*   *   *

It is such fun having Betsy here with me. She is so bright and amusing, quite different to the demure little mouse who first entered these doors.

I give orders for Miss Ostrey to come up to the house for fittings, and once she has gone, Betsy imitates her strange walk and the way she has of poking forward to look closely at things. Miss Ostrey has a limp, poor dear, and doubtless her eyesight has been impaired by too much sewing. It is not kind to make fun of her, but Betsy is so amusing, sticking out her rear and pushing her head out before her, moving crab-like across the room, that I am forced to laugh outright and cannot scold her. She has a talent for mimicry, my Betsy, and I

28

have not laughed for a long time. Since—when? I wonder.

I tell Miss Ostrey firmly that we do not require more than two plain garments, the other four dresses must be of velvet for the winter months, and two of muslin for the summer.

Fortunately I have small feet even though I am tall, and Betsy is already making use of two pairs of slippers which I seldom wear. She has also received a pair of my button boots for outside walking. There are more than enough shawls and night-gowns and petticoats for the two of us, and I have enjoyed myself more than I would have thought possible a month back. It is rather like having a younger sister to spoil, and anything which makes Betsy happy pleases me.

It is a pity that the other servants do not care for her. They must be jealous of our relationship, and though I try to be pleasant and friendly towards them all I am not at ease in their company, whereas with Betsy I am totally relaxed and carefree.

Helen does not like her in the nursery but that is understandable; Charlie dotes on my new companion, and even I must stay in the background when Betsy appears.

'I have always loved children,' Betsy tells me, after a noisy frolic with my son. 'Mother had three more little ones after me and it was a great sadness when they died.' Her hair has fallen from its neat bun and tumbles about her shoulders, having been ruthlessly tugged by Charlie's insistent fingers. And her cheeks are pink, making her look most attractive.

'You should wear your hair loose, Betsy,' I say, admiring her small excited face. 'We must use curling tongs to give you some curls—they would suit you.'

'Oh, ma'am, 'twould not be seemly.' She lifts her arms and tries to pin her hair up.

Helen flings a spiteful glance in our direction and carries a screaming Charlie into the far room.

'Oh, dear, now we have upset the baby—'

'And his nurse-maid,' says Betsy, smiling. 'What a plain creature she is, to be sure, but no doubt she cares for your son adequately. Dearie me, I am in a state, we'd best go below, ma'am, and I shall neaten myself up before lunch.'

I do not know what Mr Hawton thinks of Betsy Potter. He is such a quiet, controlled man one can never guess his feelings. She joins us at all our meals and it has helped me to have her with us, for I can address myself to her and thus conversation is easier. But she is still very formal and correct in my husband's presence and does not show her true self at all. I see him glancing at me from time to time, and, as I am obviously in good spirits now that Betsy has replaced Mrs Beadle, he seems well satisfied. I ask him about his day and how the

30

affairs of the estate are running because I know Betsy will be interested, and I want to prove to her that not all landowners are as uncaring as the one she knew as a child. Then Mr Hawton enquires about our day and the once-dreaded mealtimes pass swiftly and pleasantly.

This evening my husband tells me that he is off to London once again.

'You will be all right, Miranda?' he queries, when he comes to bid me goodnight. 'You seem satisfied with your new companion so I can leave you with an easy mind?'

'That you may, sir.' I lie back upon my pillows and sigh contentedly. 'Betsy is an amiable girl and I am becoming most fond of her. I am so pleased that you decided to engage her—she makes me happy.'

A strange expression crosses his face, then is gone. 'I am glad,' he answers, coming forward to kiss me briefly. 'I want you to be happy, my dear, and content. If there is anything you desire whilst I am away let Mrs Wanstead know, and she will see that your wishes are carried out. Does Betsy ride?'

'No! She is frightened of horses, but I intend getting her up on Mary before the month is out.'

'Then be sure to take Old George with you when you go out on Cloud. You are not to ride alone, Miranda, is that understood?'

'Yes.' I stare up at his sombre face. It is

frustrating not to be able to gallop freely across the land—Old George is a careful rider and both Cloud and I find his company irksome. But my husband is far too severe a man to be disobeyed. 'I doubt that I shall ride much during your absence. Betsy likes to walk and wishes to see everything on this place.'

'Home,' Mr Hawton says quickly, 'this is your home, Miranda, and it would be a good idea to get to know it better.'

'Where was my home before?' I ask, watching for the anger which I know will instantly appear in his eyes.

Impatience flares briefly as he looks down at me, then all emotion is masked. Why does he have to be so controlled all the time? No wonder our relationship is strained, we are never natural or at ease in each other's company.

'I do not know where your home is, Miranda, and that is the truth. I hide what is necessary from you, but there is a great deal I do not know myself. Now, go to sleep and think about the future. I shall not be away for more than two weeks. Perhaps Betsy will have had her first riding lesson by the time I return.'

I watch him walk to the door, a tall, proud figure, totally in command of all of us here at Hazelwood.

*   *   *

The day after Mr Hawton departs Betsy announces that we are to go visiting.

'We will begin on the east side of the estate,' she says briskly, 'and see what is needed and have a nice little chat. The fresh air and exercise will do us good, and 'tis time your husband's tenants got to know their mistress.'

I am hesitant. The idea of calling upon strangers is frightening and I am not sure that Mr Hawton would approve.

'Can we not speak to Mr Cross, the steward?' I suggest. 'He will know if it is a good idea and advise us accordingly.'

'Nonsense.' Betsy is already pulling on her boots. 'You are the mistress here and you give the orders. I have already told Mrs Wanstead that you will be requiring a pot of good bone broth and two loaves this morning. "Madam will be calling on the poor," I told her. She did not like me telling her what to do and ruffled up like an old hen. "Not necessary," she muttered, loud enough for me to hear. Silly old woman! She lives here with her warm parlour and full stomach, nicely cared for—I don't suppose she knows what it is like to be hungry.' Betsy stands up, wrapping one of my shawls about her shoulders and straightening her bonnet. 'Come along, we'll go down to the kitchen now. Your presence there might make all the servants work a bit harder.'

'Betsy,' I say, 'you must not assume that all landowners are like that one who mistreated

33

your father. I am sure Mr Hawton is a very good man and that all his people are well cared for.'

'Maybe, but that is exactly what we are going to find out.' And she leads the way downstairs with the light of battle in her pale eyes.

*   *   *

We return from our morning's adventure in sober mood, for I am shocked by what I have seen and Betsy is defiantly triumphant.

We saw but three cottages, hovels, more like, with mud-covered floors and sacking at the broken windows. In one the roof had partially collapsed, forcing the family to live in the lower room. Seven of them, parents, grandmother, and four children, eat and sleep in that cramped space. I could not believe it and found the few minutes spent in each abode the most uncomfortable of my known life.

Betsy was wonderful, talking and soothing, handing out the bread and soup as if she were the lady of the manor, whilst I stood speechless and upset behind her, appalled by the stench and the sights which assaulted my senses.

And ten shillings a week! That was all that the father brought home after a week's labouring. And when Betsy asked how this was spent the answer was—'On flour, yeast and candles.'

What a meagre existence! Betsy was right, so right! I cannot wait now to see my husband again and make him do something about those terrible conditions. Betsy says I should speak to Mr Cross at once, but I shrink from such action. It is not for me to give orders to the steward. We must wait for Mr Hawton to return and do what we can, meanwhile, to ease such suffering. Tomorrow we are to move on to the cottages further down the lane, though heaven knows what poverty we have yet to discover.

Betsy says little, but her mouth is tight and she is no longer my gay companion of yesterday. We eat our lavish meal in silence, and the meat and rich gravy stick in my throat as I remember what we have lately seen; the children tearing at the bread with teeth and fingers, and the old grandmother, too weak to do more than raise her head as Betsy held the bowl of broth to her lips.

As I rise to go upstairs for my afternoon nap, Mrs Wanstead appears in the doorway of the dining-room, an extraordinary expression on her round face.

'We have visitors, ma'am,' she says, twisting her hands together in front of her apron, 'and Rose has shown them into the drawing-room.'

'Visitors!' Betsy and I stare from opposite sides of the table. 'Who are they, Mrs

Wanstead? Do you know them?'

She nods. 'One of them. She came here a very long time ago. It is Mr Hawton's mother, ma'am, accompanied by a Miss Somerset.'

'Mr Hawton's mother!' Dear heavens, that such a thing should happen when he is away from home! And I did not know that he had a mother. He only told me once about the brother who died, the elder brother, from whom he had inherited Hazelwood.

'Betsy!' I turn to stare in anguish at my companion. 'What am I to do?'

'You are to go in there and introduce yourself. Keep calm and remember that you are the mistress of Hazelwood and they are your guests. Offer them refreshment, ma'am, and hope that they will soon go.'

Mrs Wanstead shakes her head. 'They have brought boxes with them and intend staying the night, ma'am, or even longer,' she whispers, and my heart flutters in panic.

'Go *on*,' says Betsy fiercely, 'go and greet them. And be proud. You are Mr Hawton's wife—now lift your head and show courage.'

She comes round to my side of the table and pushes me towards the door.

'Come with me, Betsy, I cannot face them alone.'

'Very well.' She falls into step behind me, and we follow Mrs Wanstead's buxom form across the hall and into the drawing-room.

Standing by the window overlooking the

drive is a tall, silver-haired lady, beautifully attired in a gown of grey silk. There are diamonds at her throat and on her long nervous hands, and she has the same dark eyes as her son, the same jutting nose.

Mrs Wanstead announces us and then scurries away.

'Well.' The lady turns from the window and moves forward towards the couch where a fair-haired young woman is sitting. 'And since when has Robert had a wife?'

She fingers the jewels at her throat, and her dark eyes travel over my face and body in a most impolite fashion.

'We were married in Hertford—' I begin.

'And why was I not informed? Why this secrecy?'

'You must ask Mr Hawton that.'

'Indeed I will. Where is he? Send word that I wish to see him at once. Dear me, Cynthia, this is all quite outrageous.' She turns to her companion. 'No wonder Robert broke off all contact with me and has been so difficult to find. Doubtless he is ashamed of this union and thus hides the woman away in the country.' She faces me again. 'Why have you not sent word for my son?'

'He is not here, he has gone to London.'

She is silent for a moment. 'Then would you kindly dismiss that person behind you, I do not care to have servants listening to my conversation.'

I nod at Betsy, who bobs a curtsey and withdraws. But anger is beginning to burn in my breast, anger and indignation at being spoken to in such a presumptuous manner. I stare at the younger lady on the couch.

'Perhaps you would introduce me, ma'am?'

'This is Miss Cynthia Somerset, a distant relative, and one whom I love as dearly as a daughter.'

I bow at Miss Somerset, who looks back at me with interest, her eyes on my scar.

'Would you care for some refreshment?' I move towards the mantelpiece to summon Mrs Wanstead, but the older woman lifts her hand.

'We have eaten, thank you. Now tell me about yourself. If you are my daughter-in-law I suppose I must accept the fact, shock though it has been, and we had better get to know each other during Robert's absence.' She seats herself beside Miss Somerset, her back rigidly straight, her hands folded upon her lap. 'What was your name before you wed my son? And how did you come by that disfigurement?'

'It—it was an accident, ma'am,' I stammer.

'A fall from your horse, no doubt? What a dangerous sport it is, to be sure. When poor Simon died I told Robert—' she stops abruptly, 'but there, I digress. And your parents? What is their name?'

This, then, is what my husband has been trying to avoid. No wonder we give no parties, accept no invitations. For what can be told about Robert Hawton's wife? She does not know her name, or her age, or her family. She is a nothing person with a marred face.

'Ford,' I say, my mind working furiously, unwilling to see those eyes light up with scorn and shocked disbelief. 'I am Miranda Ford and my father owns a large estate in the north of Hertfordshire. Grove Manor,' I say, holding my hands tightly before me, feeling the rings cut into my flesh. 'Perhaps you have heard of it?'

She shakes her head, frowning a little. 'Your father is a landowner, then? Thank heavens he is not in trade. Robert showed some sense, after all. What is your father's given name?'

'Samuel, and there are five of us children, three boys and two girls. And my mother's name is Margaret.' God forbid that I shall have to go on like this all afternoon. 'Where is your home, Mrs Hawton? Have you come from far?' If she will only talk about herself it will give me some respite.

'Has Robert not told you? Dear me, what a secretive wretch he is! But always was, even as a boy. Simon was much more open, an easier, more cheerful child in every way. I never had the same feeling for Robert.' She looks across at me with those daunting eyes. 'We come from Sussex, and it was a dreadful journey— we are quite worn out although we stayed a night in London. Robert refuses to answer my letters and so I decided to come and see him

39

for myself. What a nuisance that he is not here—if I had known that he was in town I should not have troubled to venture this far north. When do you expect his return?'

'Not for some weeks.' Surely they will not remain that long? 'He had business matters to attend to.'

'Gambling, no doubt.' Miss Somerset laughs, showing pretty white teeth. 'And women!' She is a lovely creature, with pale golden hair, beguiling dimples and soft white hands. Her gown is a deep pink, with a tightly laced corsage, showing off her chemisette which is embroidered with tiny rosebuds; a white silk shawl is around her shoulders. 'Dear Robert, he loved to teach me cards but I did not care for them myself because he always won.'

'You know him well?' I stare at her thick golden hair, her unblemished complexion. With someone like this about why on earth had he chosen *me?*

'We grew up like brother and sister,' she says, 'for Ladylea was my home ever since my parents died and Aunt Edith took me to stay with her. Has Robert not told you of me, either?'

I shake my head. Ladylea. Blood begins to pound in my ears and I hear their voices from a distance. Ladylea! I know that name. Somewhere, some time in the past I have heard that name.

'Are you quite well?' Mrs Hawton is moving towards me and her face swims before my eyes. 'Cynthia, ring the bell, I think she is going to swoon.'

THREE

Ladylea. The name keeps ringing in my ears as I lie in bed whither Betsy and Mrs Wanstead have carried me. I have an appalling headache and cannot think clearly, cannot rid my mind of swirling mist and throbbing pain. But that one word is definite—I know beyond doubt that it is familiar. Ladylea . . .

Think. Think back—force yourself to go back in time. Where did you live before coming to Hertford? The Ram Inn was at the end of a journey. Vaguely I remember a coach journey and I was tired, so tired and aching, I cannot know for how long the jolting and discomfort lasted. But we came from somewhere—we? Mr Hawton and I. For he was my companion, that I do know.

And there was an elderly woman, not Mrs Wanstead or Mrs Beadle, but kind and soft-spoken, with a country woman's weathered complexion. Was she my mother? An aunt, perhaps? And she looked after me when I was sick. Yes, that is it! She and Ladylea are connected. I lived there. Struggling to a sitting position I clasp my head with my hands. Think, you fool!

A small cottage, dark and cramped, but not dirty—not like the ones here on the estate. There was warmth and cleanliness and good food there, and gentle hands washing me, and the same hands feeling my head and anointing a soothing balm. Yes, I do remember. And a man, too, an elderly man, who tiptoed into my room from time to time and brought little posies of wild flowers which he placed in an earthenware jug beside my bed. They were the first things I saw when I awoke each morning. And Mr Hawton, he was there too, sometimes. Not my husband then, for we were married later in Hertford. But he visited me in that cottage . . .

I lie back exhausted, so much thinking has wearied me beyond belief. But they are coming, the thoughts and memories. Why was I so ill? From the wound, of course, the head wound.

Betsy peers round the door.

'Ah, you are awake at last. I'll ring for some tea. How are you feeling now, ma'am? You gave us all a great shock, you did.'

'Tired. But I know that place, Betsy, I know Ladylea.'

'Ladylea? What ever is that?'

'It is where Mrs Hawton comes from, and where I came from also. If only Mrs Hawton were a more sympathetic person I should like to talk to her.'

'What about that Miss Somerset? She seems friendly enough.' Betsy lifts my head and plumps up the pillows. 'Been up to the nursery to see Charlie this afternoon, they have, and

Mrs Hawton is delighted with her grandson. Wants to take him home with her, she says.'

'What!' I sit up so abruptly that the action jolts my neck and my head begins a fierce tattoo. 'Betsy, give me some powders with my tea—I cannot bear this pain. She must not take Charlie away—I will not allow it!'

'There, there, it would only be for a visit. It's right for a child to see his grandmother and she has seen nothing of Charlie so far.'

'No, he is mine!' The one person that really belongs to me, the only being of my very own. 'She has no right to take him without my permission. Oh, why does Mr Hawton not return—he would never allow it.'

'Maybe that is why she wants Charlie, it will force Mr Hawton to visit her. He is not a very dutiful son by the sound of it.'

'With a mother like that who can blame him? My powders, Betsy, quickly. I must get up and speak to her.'

But I do not see Mrs Hawton again. The powders ease the pain in my head but also make me drowsy, and, with all the excitement and strain of the day, I slip back into sleep without rising from my bed. By the next day Betsy announces that Mrs Hawton and her companion have departed, taking my son and his nursemaid with them.

The days pass so slowly, I am desperate for my husband's return; the moment he comes he must drive down to Sussex and bring Charlie back. I cannot bear to go upstairs and see the empty rooms; his cot stands neat and tidy and unused in the corner of that white silent room, and no sound of childish laughter or rebellious screaming fills the air.

I am nervous and irritable and Betsy is also upsetting me. Her new gowns have been delivered and she is forever dressing up, trying on my jewellery, asking if this suits her, if that looks right. Her favourite occupation is to get out my jewel-box and rummage about with the pieces, looking like a little girl with her large wondering eyes and inquisitive fingers. Usually I am amused by her antics, but now her behaviour vexes me and I can only think about Charlie.

My continual depression seems to annoy her, too, so that we are not the contented companions of a few days ago.

'Why go on in such a way, ma'am? The boy will be well looked after—his grandmother dotes on him and you need not fear that she will illtreat him.'

That is not what I fear; I am afraid that he will grow to love her too much, that he will forget about me.

'She had no right,' I moan, making my head ache again. 'I cannot eat or sleep. I want Charlie back here in his rightful place at Hazelwood.'

'Now, now,' Betsy sighs, and begins removing the earrings and necklace which she had been admiring on herself. 'Don't start again, ma'am. Shall I sleep with you tonight? Mr Hawton will not thank me if he returns to find you red-eyed and miserable.'

'No, thank you, Betsy, I should sleep even worse with you in my bed.' I half smile at the preposterous idea. 'This is not one of those poor hovels where everyone must share the same sleeping space.'

'I only thought you might be lonely without your husband,' she answers huffily. ' 'Twas kindly meant, ma'am, and your nights must be lonely now that Mr Hawton has been gone for over a week.'

Slowly I turn to prop myself up on one elbow, my tears forgotten. 'Mr Hawton has his own room through there, as well you know.'

'His own room, of course, but he must share your bed on occasion, ma'am.' She giggles and turns away from my stare. 'I always think the gentry are fortunate in having several bedrooms to themselves. It must help with—with the having of babies, if you'll excuse me, ma'am. My poor mother was never free of Father, and the babies kept on coming even though they didn't live, poor dears.'

'I don't know what you are talking about.' Such thoughts have never crossed my mind. What have sleeping arrangements to do with producing children? I feel hot and uncomfortable—there is something strange here—Betsy is looking at me with an odd

46

expression on her face.

'I mean, when a man and woman love each other—you must understand that! Oh, don't get all prim and proper with me, ma'am, I am a farmer's daughter, remember? And you and Mr Hawton have a fine young son. How did that happen without kissing and cuddling? There, I shan't embarrass you further. Forgive me for bringing up such a private matter, but it was well meant, ma'am.'

Kissing and cuddling! My heart hammers beneath my night gown as Betsy moves about, tidying the room. I scarcely hear her as she wishes me good night. Mr Hawton has never cuddled me in my life, and he only kisses me briefly on the forehead before going to his own room. To think that she imagines that we share a bed. Revolting thought! Yet how do babies materialise? In desperation I realise that I have no idea at all. But I gave birth to Charlie, I remember that event quite well, with Dr Ingram and the village midwife working over me and helping me through that painful affair. I have, indeed, produced a child but that is the limit of my knowledge. What was it Miss Somerset said? Something about women? Does that mean that my husband goes to London in order to kiss and cuddle other females? Dear heavens—there is so much I need to know, yet whom can I ask? It will be embarrassing to talk to Betsy and humiliating to show my ignorance. But how can I learn without asking questions?

'Ma'am,' says Betsy to me next day, looking fresh and bright-eyed after a good night's sleep, whilst I lie pale and inert upon my bed, having slept little. 'Ma'am, I have been thinking about your difficult position—having no memory—and I wondered what we could do about it. You do want to remember, don't you?'

'I suppose so.' My brain is sluggish and confused from lack of sleep.

'Well, you have heard me speak of Adam Rushmore, the parson's second son? He has written me a letter asking if he might pay me a visit. Now, if you allowed him to come, ma'am, I'm thinking that he might be the very one to help you.'

'How can anyone help me to remember?'

She draws a chair up beside my bed and leans forward confidentially. 'Adam could act on your behalf, ma'am. He could go where you cannot go and ask the questions you never could. You said that the name Ladylea meant something to you, well, why can't Adam go down to Sussex and make enquiries for you?'

'I don't know—give me time.' It is quite a new idea and for the moment it takes my mind off my depressed and futile state, and my longing for Charlie. 'Would he do such a thing for me, Betsy? Why should he bother?'

'He would need payment, of course,' she

answers quickly, 'they are a poor family, and the parson would be pleased to have less mouths to feed for a while, and you would be providing employment for Adam. He is a good lad, I can vouch for that, and it would give him an interest in life. His father wants him to go into the church but Adam has no desire for such a life. Yet he must earn a living. If he travelled south for you it would widen his knowledge of the countryside, and he would meet and talk to people, which he enjoys. He has great charm, has Adam.'

'He would be discreet? I am not sure if it is a good idea.'

'Of course he will be careful. You must meet him yourself, ma'am, and tell him exactly what you want him to do. Naturally he will be discreet—I do not believe Mr Hawton would be pleased if he found out.'

No, my husband would not approve of the idea. Having hidden me away for over a year he doubtless considers that my secret is safe from the world. But that is the trouble. It is *my* secret, *my* life, he is playing with; has any person the right to withhold knowledge from the one most concerned? Perhaps. If the knowledge is painful, or unpleasant. What a decision to have to make! Of course I want to know the truth about myself, but what if the truth is too harsh to bear? Perhaps my husband is doing me a favour in denying me a past?

'You have a right to know,' says Betsy firmly. 'You are not a pet or a toy. You are a person, ma'am, and every human being has the right to know their proper name and the details of their family and background.'

'If I could meet Adam—' I begin doubtfully.

'I shall write today.' Betsy jumps up and runs to the cupboard. 'You must get dressed and face the day, ma'am. You have been lying there all white and sad for too long. We'll walk down to the village to post my letter this afternoon, and call in on the vicarage on our way home.'

'Why the vicarage? I do not care for Parson Andrews.'

'Because he is going to help us, too. I did not think it would do to have any visitors here, but when I was talking to Parson last Sunday after the service, I said that one of my family would like to come over and see me, and he kindly said that they could put up at the vicarage. I told him that Adam was my brother. Only a small half-truth, ma'am, for we were brought up like brother and sister, after all. So we'll go and make arrangements for Adam this afternoon.'

Still feeling a trifle apprehensive about Betsy's plan, knowing that Mr Hawton will be dreadfully angry if he ever finds out, I yet allow Betsy to dress me and go down to breakfast with a pleasurable excitement in my heart. Once again I am thankful that Betsy

50

Potter has come to Hazelwood. Nothing exciting ever happened with Mrs Beadle, and I am beginning to come alive, doing things I would never have dreamed of doing a few months back.

Betsy also asks me to invite Parson Andrews to dinner.

'It will do us both good to have a visitor,' she states, 'we live here together like two old crones and it will help to take your mind off Charlie until Mr Hawton returns.'

Parson Andrews is invited for Thursday evening, and he is as ingratiating and pompous as ever. But Betsy appears to find him amusing company. He tucks into Cook's excellent meal of roast beef and apple pie, and when we retire to the drawing-room, Betsy tells him about the cottages and their pitiful inhabitants. Strangely, the clergyman is not the champion for her cause which she was no doubt expecting. Is it because he needs my husband's patronage? Or does he really believe the explanation which he gives us?

'Could you not have a word with Mr Hawton, sir, and plead with him for better conditions?' begs Betsy. 'Their plight is dreadful and it would surely not cost much to rebuild their dwellings?'

'Ah, now, Miss Potter—you are a young lady with a kind heart, I perceive,' replies the portly gentleman, leaning back in his chair and crossing his legs. 'But what thinks Mrs Hawton of the matter? She has been silent so far. Tell me your views on the matter, dear ma'am, if you will?'

'I feel the same way as Betsy does and intend speaking to my husband when he returns home.'

How I dislike the clergyman's fruity voice, and his bulbous eyes which pop out at me from his red face. He obviously fills his belly regularly and does not know hunger; his waistcoat is too tight and his hands are short-fingered and plump.

Parson Andrews gazes at the ceiling in pious contemplation. 'What we must not forget, dear ladies, is the fact that the Good Lord made us all and that there is a rightful place for everyone here on earth. No doubt in the Kingdom of Heaven all men will be equal, but here—' and he sighs—'here we have the rich and the poor, the sick and the healthy, the wise and the foolish. Some of us are born to serve and others to command, and there is nothing a mere mortal can do to change the order of things. We cannot understand the Lord's will, but must simply accept life's diversities until we come to that blessed Kingdom where the truth will be revealed to us.'

'Does that mean you will not help us?' I query impatiently. We have to sit through lengthy sermons every Sunday, I do not wish for more preaching in my own home.

'It means, dear lady, that we have to educate them.' His eyes roll in my direction and I sense that dislike is mutual. 'As you must be aware, I am supervising the building of a school in the village—a costly business, I fear, and one in which your husband has taken an interest, a most generous interest.'

So if Mr Hawton spends money on the labourers' cottages there will be less for you? I think silently.

'First the poor must be taught—taught to think and act in a civilised manner. Then they will be able to appreciate better living conditions.'

'But who will go to this school?' asks Betsy. 'From what I know of farm life the children are put to work at a very early age. The boys go to work in the fields and the girls are expected to help in the home almost as soon as they can walk.'

'Schooling must be made compulsory,' answers the clergyman. 'It is only through education that a man can hope to better himself.'

'Then higher wages are essential,' says Betsy, 'for nobody is going to send a boy to school when he can be out earning a few pence for his family on the land.'

'Why not let the gentlemen worry about such matters,' says our companion jovially, 'such problems are not for pretty little heads like yours. By all means speak to your husband, Mrs Hawton, if what you have lately seen has distressed you. But I think that he and Mr Cross are best equipped to deal with such issues. Ladies are better suited to needlework and piano-playing and, dare I say it, flower-arranging in the church?'

'I should like to be of use, sir,' Betsy dimples, 'I always arranged the flowers at home and would be glad to lend a hand.'

'Then if Mrs Hawton can spare you for an hour, or so, every Saturday morning, I should be more than grateful for your assistance, Miss Potter.'

I nod at Betsy's eager glance. If she wishes to spend time in that dark little church, good luck to her. The building depresses me, and the one-and-a-half hours spent within its walls on a Sunday are enough for me.

*　　*　　*

Mr Hawton has returned and departed again. He was furious, as I knew he would be, and has travelled down to Sussex to retrieve our son. He does not often show his emotions, but his mouth clamped shut when I told him the news, and his brows drew down over his dark eyes in a very fierce manner.

'Your mother did not even ask permission,' I told him, glad to see him react in such a way. 'I was unwell for a few days and before I could recover she had gone, taking Charlie with her.'

54

'I shall travel down to Sussex at once. She had no right to act in such high-handed fashion. Did you speak much with her, Miranda?' He was surveying me closely, worried about the mention of Ladylea, perhaps?

'We spoke but a few words together,' I told him. 'I was so surprised and put out by their visit that I did not act the part of hostess very graciously.'

'They?' he queried. 'Who was with Mother?'

'A Miss Somerset.' I watched his face. 'She said she knew you well.'

'Cynthia.' He turned his back on me and walked over to the window. 'She is still there, then? I would have thought she'd be wed by now.'

Why had Mr Hawton not married Miss Somerset, I thought suddenly. She was a very lovely lady and they had grown up together. She also looked as if she would know how to kiss and cuddle, with her soft white skin and golden hair. Reddening at the thought I put her firmly from my mind.

'Please bring Charlie back. He will not understand why he has been taken away, and I always used to go up and play with him every evening. He will not know what has happened—I cannot bear to think that he might be crying for me and I am not there.'

Mr Hawton came swiftly back across the

room. 'I will go this afternoon, Miranda, do not fear. And I shall not return without him.' He took my hands in his and his dark eyes, so like his mother's, glowed with anger. 'You know I would never see you hurt. I am only sorry that I was not at home to greet them; this situation would never have occurred had I been present.'

His hands were warm and compelling, making me shiver and pull away from his grasp. 'Thank you, sir, I know you will not disappoint me. Please go quickly and bring Charlie back to where he belongs.'

FOUR

Adam has arrived. And what a delightful person he is! I never knew a man could be such good company. He is quite small, no taller than I am, with curly light brown hair and the merriest blue eyes. Betsy and I are so enjoying his visit—it makes me wonder how we managed before. And the best part of all is that Adam likes to ride. I have been neglecting poor Cloud of late, for Betsy refuses to go near the stables, and I do not like to leave her alone whilst I go out. But this afternoon she wanted to visit Hertford, and Parson Andrews kindly offered to take her there in his trap. So off they have gone drawn by a smart little grey, and that leaves Adam and me free for a few hours.

Cloud is swiftly saddled, along with Mr Hawton's big hunter, Brave Boy, but Old George is not happy about the arrangement.

'The master said you was not to go out without me,' he tells me grumpily.

'Mr Hawton said that I was not to ride alone, George. Now I have Mr Potter to accompany me so that is in order.'

'And he won't like a stranger riding Boy, neither.'

'Don't be such a cross-patch! Boy hasn't been ridden properly for weeks and he is longing for a good gallop. Come, Adam, let us go before we waste more time.'

'And heavy-handed,' mutters Old George, as we pass him, 'ruin the horse's mouth, he will. And what will the master say then?'

We leave him mumbling to himself, and I feel at once gloriously free, as if I have been let out of gaol. Yet I have grown fond of Hazelwood. The house is too big and too sombre for my liking, but it will be different when Charlie is older and running around the spacious rooms, bringing them to life; and the servants are willing and well-trained by Mrs Wanstead. The main problem is that I am lonely, living with a man who is so distant in manner, so difficult to know well, and who, moreover, is often away in London. But life improved when Betsy came to stay and now, with Adam proving such an entertaining and easy companion, I am suddenly happy, despite Charlie's absence, and feel absurdly gay and carefree.

'Tell me,' Adam says, as we pause to rest the horses at the top of the rise, 'tell me how much you know, Lady Dreamer.' He looks across at me and laughs. 'I cannot call you Miranda, it would be too presumptuous, and Mrs Hawton sounds stiff and unfriendly. For you are my friend, are you not? I feel a kinship with you, though we are not related. At least, I presume not!' His blue eyes crinkle and his wide mouth curves in amusement. 'Who knows where you belong? We must indeed unravel this mystery. Tell me, Lady Dreamer, what are your earliest memories?'

'Of being ill,' I answer slowly, gazing down across the park-land towards the house, which looks small from this distance, but red-bricked and secure, sheltered by the rambling outbuildings on the one side and the stalwart elms which border the garden on the other. 'I must have been ill for a long while for I spent so much time in bed; in a cottage tended by an elderly couple. Once or twice I walked out in a narrow sheltered garden—Mr Hawton visited me there—but I don't remember going for walks, or seeing a village, or anything else.'

'And Ladylea?'

'Nothing, save that I know the name.'

'And you believe it to be a house?'

I nod.

'Yet Mrs Hawton did not appear to recognise you when she came here?'

'I am sure she did not know me before, neither she nor Miss Somerset did. And I did not feel that I knew them, not like I knew the name Ladylea.'

'The key must lie there.' Adam sits in thought for a while and there is silence save for the far trilling of a lark overhead and the munching of the horses as they graze.

'You want me to go down to Sussex and visit Ladylea?' Adam looks across at me. 'Have you any idea where the place is?'

'No, but talk to the grooms. You won't get anything out of Old George but the other lads must know something. Mrs Hawton arrived by carriage so her horses must have been tended in our stables for those few days.'

'And there is no one else around here to whom I can go for information? Who was your companion before Betsy? What about Parson Andrews, or the doctor? Have they been told nothing about you?'

I shake my head. 'Mr Hawton brought me here from Hertford as his bride, and that is all that anyone knows. My husband is—he is a very close man, you see, not given to gossip or confidences. When the parson calls they discuss village matters and the building of the new school, for which Parson Andrews is always begging money. And Dr Ingram is as puzzled as I am. Mr Hawton is very short with him and has only said that I am recovering from a severe illness and must have frequent supplies of powders for my headaches. Mr Hawton wants me to think only about the future, he says the past is best forgotten.'

'Strange.' Adam pulls at Boy's head and kicks him on to a walk. 'I could understand it all better if neither of you knew about your past, if he had met you since your loss of memory. But that your husband knows and will not tell you—that I find exceeding odd.'

'Mrs Beadle has gone away to her sister,' I say, moving Cloud up beside him, 'and I am certain that she knows nothing for my husband only engaged her services when we came to Hertford; she was waiting for us at the inn.' I frown. 'It was another woman in Sussex, a motherly soul who nursed me most tenderly, yet I cannot think of her name.'

'It will take time,' Adam remarks, 'you realise that I cannot act in haste? I shall first have to find Ladylea, then live somewhere in that area and get to know the local people, allow them to talk to me. Country folk do not take kindly to strangers who come asking questions.'

'I do realise that and beg you to be discreet. Mr Hawton must not hear of your investigation and now, with this contact with his mother, news will spread quickly. You must not be traced back to us and please, do not use the name of Potter.'

'My name is Rushmore, Lady Dreamer, and I can use that openly for none can connect it with you.'

'What of your father's connection with my husband? In what way are they related?'

'Distantly, and only through my poor dead mother. Do not fear, Lady Dreamer, none of my family has ever been to Sussex and none will associate me with you, or Mr Hawton.'

'And payment?' I add quickly. 'Payment will be difficult for I have no money—yet you must live. How can we arrange that?'

'Have you jewellery?'

I sigh with relief. 'Of course.' Jewels I have in plenty, so many that Mr Hawton will not know if some are missing, and they mean nothing to me. The jade earrings can go, and the gold chain with the pearl pendant, and the heavy beaten gold bracelet which I have always found cumbersome upon my wrist. 'Will they do?' I say, after describing the pieces to Adam.

'Splendidly, dear madam. Now, let us forget about such mercenary talk and give these beasts the gallop they have been awaiting. I shall race you down to that hollow, Lady Dreamer, let us see who has the speediest mount.'

*   *   *

I arrive back at the house red-cheeked and exuberant, and am famished for my tea. Betsy, bless her, is already home, and Adam has returned to the vicarage.

'I hope your afternoon was as pleasant as mine,' she says, sitting serenely before the tea-trolley in my parlour. 'I invited Parson Andrews in for a cup of tea, but he has his sermon to prepare and could not spare the time.'

'He has not left many hours for such an arduous task,' I remark. 'Today is Thursday, and by the length of his normal offerings he must need a good three days to prepare himself.'

'I wish you could like him a little,' Betsy says, ringing the bell for hot water, 'he was uncommonly kind to me this afternoon and I found him a most agreeable companion.'

I grimace. 'He is too fat and his eyes are cold.'

'I grant that his looks are unattractive, but he is a most charitable gentleman. Now, enough of him. I have discovered an interesting fact and have a theory about your past, ma'am.'

'Tell me, Betsy.' Once the hot water has arrived and the maid withdrawn, we settle ourselves and begin to eat.

'I went to the church where you and Mr Hawton were married, and was able to see the book where all the entries are made. You mentioned a winter's day, ma'am, but in fact you were wed on the twentieth of April, 1840.'

'It was a bitter day—I had thought it to be mid-winter!' I laugh, but my laughter fades as I notice my companion's expression. 'Go on then, what more have you to tell me?'

'Your son, ma'am, on what date was he born?'

'I remember that day well, on the ninth of September, and a golden day it was, sunny and warm, for we had a glorious autumn last year, if you remember? But why do you look like that?'

'Because, ma'am, it takes nine months from a baby's conception to its birth,' Betsy says clearly, 'and that is the answer to part of your mystery. Either Mr Hawton and you behaved improperly and your family banished you from Sussex, so your husband-to-be bundled you up here and married you in haste; or,' she pauses dramatically, 'that babe is another man's son and Mr Hawton wed you out of pity!'

'No!' Not that—not another man—it cannot be possible when I am so vague, so uncertain about all this kissing and cuddling. I surely would never have allowed another man in my bed?

I spring up and begin to pace the room. Why do I know so little about marriage, and the begetting of children? I have lost my memory but ordinary, everyday facts remain clear in my mind. I know that there are fifty-two weeks in a year, twenty-four hours in a day; know the seasons and can recite my mathematical tables up to twelve times twelve. A mother would surely guide her daughter and teach her about life, and love and marriage. Why do I know nothing about such things? Was I an orphan? But then I would have spoken to other girls, giggled and exchanged confidences with people of my own age, would I not? There is too much lacking in me, more, much more than loss of memory.

I pace to and fro, twisting my hands, a terrible urgency welling up within my breast. 'Then why this scar? How did I receive such a head wound? Have you an answer for that,

Miss Know-all? And why did Mrs Hawton not recognise me?'

'Do not vent your wrath on me, ma'am,' says Betsy huffily, from behind the silver teapot. 'I am only trying to help. Maybe your father hit you and you fell awkwardly, gashing open your forehead.'

'I cannot imagine Mr Hawton ever acting in an improper fashion,' I say, coming back to sit opposite my companion. 'And if it were another man, why did my father not force *him* to marry me?'

'Perhaps he was already married.'

'No, Betsy, no! I cannot believe that I should have been so foolish. It is true that my past is a blank but I know *myself* and am quite certain that I would never have behaved in such a reckless manner. Never would I have gone bedding with another man.' I feel myself redden as the words stumble from my lips. 'Mr Hawton is the only man with whom—for whom I have ever had affection.'

But that affection is not normal, it seems, not complete. Yet how had Charlie appeared?

'Drink your tea and calm yourself. It is no good getting in a state and Adam will clear up all these details once he has reached Sussex.'

*   *   *

Today Adam left, taking with him various pieces of my jewellery, which he will sell in different towns on his way south. It would not do to take them all to one place to sell, for he bears a small fortune in gold and precious stones, enough to last him for many months. He has promised to go carefully, how dreadful if he should be taken for a thief and the gems traced back to Hazelwood!

We are at a loss, Betsy and I, not knowing what to do with ourselves. For up until now Adam has visited us daily, smuggled in through the side door by a giggling Betsy, and taken tea with us, hiding behind the tapestry screen when Rose brings in the tray.

It did not matter that he stayed at the vicarage, nor that we rode together once, but to have him calling regularly at the house might have given cause for gossip and I could not allow that. Betsy met him often in the village and they would walk together every day, for he was known as her brother, but I had to wait for the afternoons, and the two or three hours which we spent together were some of the happiest of my known life.

Adam and Betsy were clever at playing games and taught me how to act Charades and Dumb Crambo. I was always quicker at guessing the word games, but they were better at cards, which I found confusing. It was as if I had a family of my own, at last, and we enjoyed ourselves so much that sometimes Betsy had to hold a cushion over her face to stifle her laughter, and I had to press a handkerchief to my lips for fear that our merrymaking might be heard down in the servants' quarters.

Now Adam has gone and we have to contain ourselves in patience. He has promised to write to Betsy every week once he is settled, but it seems a long time to wait for the first news. Charlie has gone, Mr Hawton has gone, Adam has gone; how lonely we are, exactly like the two old crones which Betsy once called us.

'We must visit some more families,' she says, when I fret over my sewing and find fault with her monotonous reading. 'It's no good sitting here all day moping. I will ask Cook for more goodies and we'll go out this afternoon. Until you speak to your husband about those awful conditions, we must do our best to relieve the suffering of those poor people.'

Today we go west but it is the same story, though these families are not so welcoming and appear to resent our intrusion. One woman who answers the door is thin and spiteful and knocks the bowl of soup from Betsy's hands.

'We don't want no charity,' she shrills, placing her hands on her hips and kicking aside a small girl who has knelt to scoop up the spilt liquid with her little hands. 'Give our men better wages and we can look after ourselves. And tell Mr Cross that our roof's leaking and he promised two weeks ago to get it mended. Higher wages for our men is what we want, and you can keep your offering, lady, or feed it to the swine. Go back to your cosy fireside and joints of meat and leave us alone. Coming here, poking and prying, God knows, the Frenchies done it right. Off with their heads and let the people rule—that's what I say!'

'Martha—come away and shut the door,' calls a feeble voice from the interior, 'you've said enough, woman.'

'We are going.' Betsy lifts her skirts and turns away, her nostrils pinched in disgust. 'There are others who are only too glad to accept our charity.'

'Boot-licking worms! They don't deserve to live.'

'Betsy,' I say, pulling at her shawl, frightened by the woman's raw antagonism. 'Betsy, come.'

'And don't forget to tell Mr damned Cross about the roof. Our Mabel's got the fever and if she dies from this damp and cold I'll kill him with me bare hands, so help me!'

'Come,' I whisper, and we turn and hurry from the hovel as she continues to hurl abuse after us.

We are both shaken by the unpleasant episode and walk quickly up the lane, our basket still half-filled with provisions.

'There's another cottage over there, across the field. Do you want to try there?' I ask, sorry for Betsy, who is looking white and strained. Her action had been kindly meant.

'I'll never help another of those wretches,'

she answers through tight lips, walking very fast. 'Parson Andrews was quite right, they don't deserve pity. That slut should be whipped for her insolent behaviour.'

'She has had a hard life, and her child is sick. Comparisons must be bitter,' I say quietly. 'We have so much and she so little.'

'But I was trying to *help*,' snaps Betsy, 'why couldn't she see that?'

'Been having trouble with Martha Wright, have you?' A voice interrupts us, and I gasp and grab hold of Betsy's arm as an old woman emerges from a gap in the hedge. She is a toothless crone, with a densely wrinkled face. An old black hat is pulled forward concealing her hair, but her eyes are clear and a penetrating blue. 'Always causing trouble, that one, ever since she came from the town with her clever ideas. Dick Wright ought never to have wed her.' She smiles, exposing naked gums. 'There, there, I won't harm you. Old Mother Scurry looks an evil hag but her heart is good. Have you a little something for me in your basket, Missy? I'm not too proud to accept favours, and times is bad just now, as you've been seeing.'

In her hands is a bunch of greenery, made up of what looks like weeds and nettles. Is that all she can find to eat? I hesitate, wondering whether to help her, but Betsy places her free hand over the basket and lifts her chin in a defiant manner.

'And who might you be? Do you live on the estate?'

'Over yonder, in that cottage. You are welcome to call and take a drink with me. And you, Mistress Hawton,' she turns her gaze on me, 'come and take some dandelion tea with an old woman. I can offer you that, but no cake to go with it.'

'Let her have the basket, Betsy. We are finished now and will not see any more people in need.'

'I don't like the look of her.' Betsy does not bother to lower her voice, and I feel my cheeks redden at her hurtful words. 'Go away, old woman, and do not pester us.' And she turns and walks purposefully away.

'Betsy has been badly used,' I try to explain, 'she meant well and was insulted by that woman down there—please forgive her.'

'You have a kind heart.' The old crone comes nearer and touches my sleeve. 'But be careful, mistress, you are surrounded by evil and will need all your strength to come through.'

I take a step back, repulsed by her appearance, my heart beginning to thud with fear. 'What do you mean?'

'Any time you want to talk to Mother Scurry you come across that field and knock at my door. I shall not send you away, rest assured. But don't bring her.' She jerks her head at Betsy's retreating back. 'Come alone, mistress,

I shall help you if I can. There are dark days ahead before the light.'

'Do you know about me?' I lean forward, sensing that her wisdom is great, fascinated by her ugly face and all-seeing eyes. 'Do you know who I am?'

She nods. 'You are good—too good for such evil deeds. Beware, mistress, tread warily and keep your head.' She lifts her free hand and touches my scar lightly with her claw-like fingers. 'Poor thing, poor innocent thing.'

Then she wraps her shawl firmly around her crooked body and begins to plod across the field towards her cottage, still hugging her bundle of weeds.

'I shall come!' I call after her.

She lifts a hand in salute and I turn and begin to run after Betsy.

FIVE

Mr Hawton has returned bringing Charlie, my darling son, with him. And the babe has grown, it seems, after these few short weeks; grown older and larger and I hug him to me, holding his solid little body as if I will never let him go. Charlie laughs and pats my hair and snuggles against me. He has not forgotten!

And Helen is glad to be back, bustling about the nursery, opening and shutting drawers, packing garments and linen carefully away in their rightful places.

'It was pleasant there, ma'am, and we had a lovely sunny room for Charlie, with a little white-painted one next door for me. The master's old nursery, it was, all very comfortable and nice. And a beautiful garden, too, where we went for walks. 'Tis a lovely home, ma'am, this Ladylea.'

'And you are sorry to be home now, Helen?' I say, watching her in the mirror as she walks to and fro.

'Not sorry, no, ma'am, I like it here and didn't feel right away from Hazelwood. But I shall miss some of the people.' She blushes and ducks her head.

I am more knowledgeable, more alert, thanks to Betsy. 'Did you meet a man, Helen?'

She nods her head, her back half-turned

away from me. ' 'Twas one of the grooms, ma'am, and we got talking on one of our walks—Charlie loved the horses. And he was ever so kind, this Jake, and good to Charlie and polite to me.' She sniffs, and her right ear glows as red as her hair above her starched collar.

'Oh, Helen, I'm so glad for you. Perhaps he could come and work here? Old George is always having trouble keeping his lads, and no wonder with his surly temper. Tell me his name, Helen, and I will talk to my husband.'

'Would you really, ma'am?' She turns to face me, her eyes alight with hope. 'Jake Minns, he is, and he told me he'd like to see this part of the world. He's ever so good with horses, ma'am, and he'd work hard—I'd see he wouldn't let you down.'

'I cannot promise.' I cuddle Charlie to me, wondering if I should have said so much without first asking Mr Hawton's permission. But it is so pleasant being able to converse with the girl, so good to feel at ease in her company, I spoke without thought.

Handing Charlie back to his nurse, I realise that with my new-found confidence is growing an understanding of other people, of how they live and think and feel. Thanks to Betsy I am interested in many things now, after being both mentally and physically inert for so long.

'Oh, ma'am, I nearly forgot!' Helen settles Charlie on her hip and spins round to disappear into the farther room. Then back she comes with a letter in her hand.

' 'Twas given me by an elderly woman who lived in a cottage at the end of the drive. Her husband was the family's old coachman, and she was the master's nurse when he was a child. She asked me to give you this. Ever so fond of Charlie, she was, and wanted to tell you how proud she was of Mr Hawton's son and heir.'

I keep my face expressionless and thank the girl before leaving the room, but once outside I fly down the stairs and along the corridor to my bedroom.

With trembling fingers I open the letter.

'Dear Madam, just a short note to wish you well and say as how pleesed I was to see your son and no that you was recovered. I promised Mister Robert I wood never rite but just this once I cood not help meself. Do not tell him I rote but God bless you. I think of you evry nite in me prayers. Yours, Annie Malthouse.'

Annie! Yes, that was her name. The old man called her that—now I remember. And she had cared for me so lovingly. But she was not my mother, then, nor a relation. What on earth was I doing lying sick in her cottage, whilst Mrs Hawton lived up the drive at the big house and knew nothing about me? I was hidden even there—for God's sake, why?

But she will know, Annie will know from whence I came. The moment we hear from

Adam and have an address where he can be reached, he must be given this vital information. He must go and see Annie Malthouse and beg or bribe her to tell him the truth.

*   *   *

'There is just one thing,' says Mr Hawton, when he comes to bid me goodnight. 'Now that you have Charlie safely home again I hope you won't object.' He stands beside my bed, very tall, his face half-shadowed in the candlelight.

'What is it?'

'My mother wishes to have the boy visit her for two weeks every summer, Miranda, and she also asked if she might spend Christmas here at Hazelwood.'

I am happy now—my son and husband have returned, Adam is searching for the truth, and my life has suddenly become of interest. Surely a little compassion can be shown a lady who loves her only grandchild?

'Of course,' I nod, and a look of relief lightens my husband's countenance. 'So long as he always comes back, and she does not stay too long.'

He smiles then; he should do it more often, for it softens his features and makes him appear more sympathetic.

'Entirely my own feelings, Miranda. Mother and I do not see eye to eye on many subjects and I realise that she is a difficult woman, and I, no doubt, am a stubborn and infuriating man. But I could not refuse her these requests and hoped that you would also agree.'

'Tell me,' I say, 'when did Simon die? And for how long did he live at Hazelwood?'

Helen said that Annie Malthouse was Mr Hawton's old nurse, and talked about using my husband's old nursery at Ladylea. Yet here is a nursery, filled witl children's books, and most of the furniture and paintings which we possess belonged to Simon.

'Simon bought this estate soon after he came of age and inherited my father's money. Mother was very fond of my elder brother, but I think he found her affection overbearing and thus removed himself to Hertfordshire. Our family home in Sussex is hers until she dies, so Simon, understandably, wanted to make a new life for himself.' Mr Hawton smiles again. 'My brother was several years older than me but I was allowed to visit him occasionally without Mother, and I loved coming up here.'

'Is that why there are so many of your books in the house? The school-room must have been used by you?'

He nods. 'Simon, of course, brought a great many of his own things with him and Mother gave him more furniture and paintings for this house. I was supposed to study in the holidays, for I was still at school, but Simon was an exciting companion and little school work was

76

done. We rode, mostly, he was very keen on hunting, and that was how he met his death.' He sighs. 'His horse stumbled at a fence seven years ago and Simon went over his head and broke his neck.'

I shudder. 'Horrible.'

'Mother only came here that once, in order to take Simon's body home. But I inherited the estate from him and it makes a good home for a family. You are happy here, Miranda?' Mr Hawton watches me closely. 'You have everything you want?'

'Very happy, and I feel so well again, I have not had a headache for over a fortnight. And Betsy helps—my life is so much better since she came to stay.'

'Good.' He turns to go but I sit forward, remembering.

'Please, may I ask you something?'

Mr Hawton pauses, his brows contracting, no doubt he expects more questions about my past.

'You know Helen, Charlie's nursemaid? Well, she met a stable-lad in Sussex and they grew fond of each other. I just wondered if ever you needed another groom, if you would send for Jake Minns?'

'Lads are not easy to come by,' he replies thoughtfully, 'they all seek employment in the towns where wages are higher. I have no doubt that Old George could do with more help.' He hesitates. 'But Mother would not be pleased if

I robbed her of labour, particularly if he is good with horses.'

'Helen said he was excellent—but possibly she was prejudiced!'

'Leave the matter with me, Miranda, and I shall see what can be done. But don't expect anything to be arranged in a hurry.'

'I won't, and thank you, sir.'

I wanted to tell him about the cottagers and the poverty we had seen, and ask for better wages and living conditions for all those families. But not yet. I had made one request and would bide my time before asking again.

*   *   *

The days pass quickly and each morning I expect news from Adam, but Betsy tells me to be patient.

'He has a long way to go and must find the place first,' she says. 'Rome was not built in a day,' and she gives a wise little nod.

She is as excited as I am about Annie Malthouse's letter, though, and promises to pass on this information to Adam the moment she knows where to write.

'Perhaps I can talk to that Miss Somerset if she accompanies Mrs Hawton at Christmas,' I say. 'There is so much I want to know about Ladylea, but dare not pester my husband.'

Betsy grunts but her thoughts are elsewhere. 'May I go into Hertford this afternoon, ma'am?' she asks. 'Parson Andrews is going and has offered me a lift again.'

When Betsy was engaged it was agreed that she should have one Sunday off each month, just like Mrs Beadle did. But she is younger than my other companion, and confesses that Sundays are dreary days in town, with all the shops closed. I have not the heart to refuse her this request although it will be the second afternoon she has had free in two weeks.

'Of course you may go, Betsy, but do not lose your heart to the parson, I believe he must have taken a liking to you.'

She laughs lightly and trips away to change out of her serge and into one of her new velvet gowns. With a black lace shawl and a green bonnet decorated with a black plume, she looks most elegant, and the green brings out the colour of her eyes making them seem an enchanting emerald.

'Very smart, Betsy,' I remark, noting her pink cheeks and excited manner. Is she falling in love with the reverend gentleman? I cannot imagine how she can enjoy his company, but life must be a little dull for her in this big house, and she has made no friends amongst the servants. She has me, of course, but it is obviously nice for her to go out and about a bit and see the world beyond Hazelwood.

I am not envious, not yet, but one day when my confidence has fully returned and when, perhaps, I know the secret of my hidden life, I, too, shall venture forth beyond these grounds. At the moment I am content to remain on the estate and once Betsy departs I decide to visit Mother Scurry. Mr Hawton has only forbidden me to ride alone, he has said nothing against walking on my own, and as Mother Scurry and Betsy did not take to each other, this is a perfect opportunity to see the old woman again.

In a small basket I carry provisions from our well-stocked larder, and make my way down the lane and across the field.

I have never seen such a cluttered room. There is only one room above and one below, and if this cottage is like the others, no doubt the upstairs is uninhabitable. Mother Scurry certainly sleeps down here for there is a rough cot in one corner. There are also ornaments, stuffed birds and old tattered books; dried grasses and bunches of herbs stuffed into pots and jars; there is washing strung across the corner nearest the fire and a bubbling kettle is on the hob.

'I was expecting you.' Her blue eyes are as intent as ever and she still wears the hat. 'Come and join me in a cup of tea, Mistress.'

'I've brought you some food, which I hope will be useful.' On the table in the middle of the room I place a loaf of bread, six eggs, a packet of tea and a bag of flour.

'Kind, very kind,' she says, her eyes darting to the table. 'And real tea—now that is a luxury. I brew my own, Mistress, and you'll be tasting some in a moment, but yours will be kept for special occasions.'

'How do you manage for money?' I ask curiously, sitting myself opposite her on a three-legged stool. 'Do you live here alone?'

With no man to bring home the wages how did she survive?

Mother Scurry cackles. 'No one would dare to share my home. Frightened to death of me, they are. But they come in need, Mistress, and I exist on the pence they give me for my remedies and potions.'

'Remedies?'

'Agrimony for stomach disorders and chamomile for the digestion, and for burns and swellings. Then there is Greater Celandine for the removal of warts, and St John's wort for depression and disturbed sleep. There are many more, but I shall not tire you with further names. Farmer Hare allows me to stay here, rent free, so long as he can call on me when his sheep get the foot rot, or when his calves sicken.' She makes tea carefully in an earthenware jug and pours me a cup. 'Taste that and see how you like it.'

'It is different—but not unpleasant.'

She nods, satisfied. 'The young lads require love-potions and the girls desire rose water for their complexions, and married women call on me when they give birth, whilst others come when they do not require their unborn babes. I do well enough, you see. Folk need me although they do not like me.'

'What do you know about me?' I lean forward eagerly. 'I need your help also for I have lost my memory. Tell me who I am.'

'You are Mrs Hawton of Hazelwood.'

'Yes, yes, now. But who was I before? Where do I come from?'

She looks at me intently with her bright eyes, then holds out her hands. 'Give me your hand and tell me about yourself.'

I place one hand in hers, and her skin feels dry and wrinkled, like that on a bird's foot.

'Do you love your husband?'

'I am fond of him, naturally,' I hesitate, 'but Mother Scurry, I do not know what love is—I cannot understand myself and am so bewildered. What is the matter with me? Why do I know so little?'

Her hands tighten and her voice is hoarse. 'Do you bed with him?'

I shake my head, ashamed.

'Yet you have a child. A son, I think?'

'Yes, Charles Robert. I have produced a baby, Mother Scurry, but do not know what happened before—how it was possible—I am so perplexed.'

'Innocent,' she mutters, letting go of my hand abruptly, 'it may be—yes, perhaps.' And she rises and shuffles over to the shelf where the books are stacked. Pulling down a tome with a cloud of dust, she brings the book over to the table and flaps through the pages, breathing heavily.

I sit silently watching her. Was she crazed? 'What are you looking for? And how did you learn to read?'

'Yes, yes,' she nods, the brim of her hat almost touching the faded pages, 'it is possible, and a chance—a grand chance, indeed!' Then she comes back to me, her eyes snapping with excitement. 'What was that you said? To read, Mistress? Why, my mother taught me. A wise one, she was, and all I know was learnt from her. And my gran before that—all wise women—and knowledge handed down from generation to generation. It's in the blood, you see. Now, what can I tell you?' Her voice fades and she shuts her eyes, concentrating.

'I see a man, dearie,' she croons, 'a man is coming here and he will have the answer to your questions. He will know all about you, yes, and there is a link, a link between us. I must meet him, also. He will come.' Mother Scurry opens her eyes and they appear milky white for a moment, as if a film has been drawn over them. 'He comes from the south, dearie, and he will know everything.'

Adam! My heart pounds in my breast and I let out a sigh of relief. 'How soon? When will he be coming?'

She shakes her head. 'That I cannot tell you, but time is not important. What matters is that he will come, and when he does the truth will be revealed. Lordy, I'm weary, Mistress.' She yawns, exposing a wide, toothless cavern.

'Forgive me, I have stayed too long.' I stand up hastily and gather the folds of my shawl about me. 'Thank you for giving me hope—I shall remember your words and wait patiently.'

Mother Scurry nods, her eyes alert and a clear blue once more. 'Come and see me again, Mistress, if you have the mind. But do not tell your husband of these visits. He would not like it. Oh, dearie me, no. Mr Hawton would not be pleased if he knew that you had spoken to Mother Scurry.' Her hand shoots out and grips my wrist, surprisingly strong for one so old. 'Don't tell, Mistress, it's a secret between you and me, understand?'

'I won't tell.' If my husband would not tell me things, why should not I also have secrets from him?

'Nobody, mind. Folks resent my knowledge and we don't want trouble, do we?'

I shake my head, suddenly anxious to be out in the fresh air away from her awesome presence.

*　　　*　　　*

Two days later a letter arrives from Adam. Betsy bears it joyfully into the sunny parlour where I am sitting.

'At last, ma'am, the news for which we were waiting, and 'tis good!'

'Betsy, give me the letter—quickly!'

But she sits herself opposite me and bends forward over the closely written pages.

'He has found Ladylea and has put up at an inn nearby. He has informed the landlord that he is recovering from a serious illness and needs peace and quiet and plenty of country air. Near the Sussex Downs, he says, and perfect for walks. Later he intends buying a horse, for then he will be more independent and can cover more ground. And he has seen that Miss Somerset, ma'am, and believes that if he goes riding he will be able to make her acquaintance, and then she will introduce him to others.' She stops, her face red with excitement. 'Oh, is it not wonderful news, ma'am?'

'What more, Betsy? Does he not say anything about me?'

She lowers her head again. 'There are many big houses in the neighbourhood and he thinks that you probably come from one of them. But he will need more money shortly.' She pauses. 'Oh, dear, it seems that he will have to pass as a gentleman of means, ma'am, in order to mix with the gentry.' Betsy looks up uncertainly. 'I suppose he will require new clothes, and the horse will be costly. Can you manage to help him again, ma'am?'

'I shall have to. I still possess some fine gems and they mean nothing to me.' Far more important is the truth about my past. 'But how can I send them, Betsy? I would not dare trust the mail.'

'I wonder.' My companion leans back in her chair, deep in thought. 'If Adam could get up to London I should not mind travelling to meet him there.'

'Betsy, how brave! Would you travel all that way on your own? I do not know if it would be wise—a young girl like you, journeying alone.'

She gives a determined nod. 'If Adam tells me where to go and is there to meet me off the coach, I could manage it. And 'twould be an experience, ma'am, I have always longed to see the city for myself.'

'But what will we tell Mr Hawton? Your absence must be explained.'

'We'll say that my mother is ill, that I must go to her. I shall only be away for a few days.'

'You will be tempting Fate, Betsy—it is a foolish thing to do.'

'Do you want to see this through, or not?' asks my companion impatiently. 'Adam and I both want to help you but we cannot progress if you become chicken-hearted about the whole affair.'

'Very well, Betsy,' I say stiffly, disliking her tone. 'If you have the courage for such an adventure, of course I shall aid you. And don't forget to tell Adam about Annie Malthouse when you write. He may have more news when you see him.'

Two weeks later Betsy departs for London,

and how long and boring are the days as I wait for her return. To the Strand, she goes, to meet Adam at Charing Cross, and I give her my ruby ring and the matching necklace, also half-a-year's wages in advance which I have begged from my husband. I give her a note for Adam, in which I thank him for what he is doing and add that I hope to see him myself in the near future.

Whilst Betsy is away I ride out daily with Old George, moving at a sedate pace beside him, remembering Adam and our wild, thrilling gallop across the park. Was he visiting those big houses under some pretext or other? Was he becoming acquainted with the families? Was he, perhaps, already in possession of my rightful name and background, and passing the information on to Betsy even now?

For three days I wait, and then on the afternoon of the fourth Betsy returns.

'I know most of it now, ma'am, and what a romantic tale it is, to be sure!' She is wearing a bonnet lined with watered silk, and her kid gloves are new, and there is a cameo brooch at her throat. She looks a most elegant and well set-up young woman. Betsy blushes as she sees me staring. 'The bonnet and gloves were paid for from my wages, ma'am, I could not resist them. The shops in London are out of this world! But Adam bought me the brooch as a keepsake of my first visit to town. He did not waste your money, I do assure you, he has a little of his own.'

'I understand. Do not imagine that I criticise, but Betsy, take off your outer garments and come and talk to me properly—I cannot wait any longer to hear your news.'

She removes her bonnet and shawl, then comes to sit before me. 'What a journey!' Betsy blows out her cheeks. 'And a dirty place it is, too, but ever so exciting. And all the people happy because of the little prince's birth. Have you heard the news, ma'am? Our Queen has produced a son, on the ninth, it was—'

'Yes, yes,' I say impatiently, 'Mr Hawton told me.'

'And Adam found a nice clean lodging-house, he was putting up at an inn nearby, and I stayed there the three nights, ma'am, and what a lot there was to see.'

'All right, all right, tell me about London later. What did you find out about me?'

'You were Miss Lavinia Montgomery,' announces Betsy solemnly, 'and your family own The Hall, near Lewes. Mr Montgomery is a widower, and you are his only child. Now, he is a selfish and miserly gentleman if you'll excuse me, ma'am, and apparently he wanted to keep you with him always. He was dead against you marrying and leaving home, you see. But one day you met Mr Robert Hawton, and 'twas love at first sight for you both.'

I sit forward, my eyes fixed on her face,

scarce believing what I hear. Lavinia Montgomery. What a stylish name. It does not sound like me at all.

'And my head? How did I get this scar and lose my memory?'

'I'm coming to that. Adam says that as there was no hope of marriage, and you were under age anyway, you and Mr Hawton decided to elope. As in all the best romances, you climbed out of your bedroom window at midnight and Mr Hawton waited below, with his horse and carriage hidden behind some trees. But you slipped, ma'am, and fell heavily, hurting your head. Mr Hawton gathered you up in his arms, took you to his carriage, and drove away to his old nurse's cottage where he knew you would be safely tended.'

'Annie Malthouse,' I breathe, 'so that is how she knows about me.'

'She was sworn to secrecy, and she hid you until you were better and able to make the journey to Hertford.'

'I can't believe it!' A wicked, cruel father, a wild romance—could I have been so dashing, so madly in love? It is as if Betsy is relating the dramatic adventure of a stranger. I shift in my chair, frowning in bewilderment. 'Is Adam certain about all this? Why did Mr Hawton not tell his mother about me?'

'Romeo and Juliet, ma'am, the Montagues and Capulets all over again. Years ago the Montgomerys quarrelled with the Hawtons, and neither family has spoken, or seen each other since. Marriage between you would have been unthinkable. And it is true. Adam traced the old nurse before he heard from me, and when she heard why he was down in Sussex, and from whom he came, she told him the whole story.'

'So Charlie is Mr Hawton's son,' I say with relief.

Betsy nods. 'You both behaved improperly, ma'am.' Her pale eyes glint with amusement. 'And it must have been quite a worry for Mr Hawton to get you well enough to wed before the baby came!'

'That will do, thank you, Betsy,' I say coldly. 'I was doubtless very young and foolish, and with no mother to tell me about such things, I suppose I was very innocent.'

'Yes, ma'am,' she replies, tucking in her chin and lowering her eyes so that I cannot read their expression.

Feeling uncomfortable that she should know so much about my past, I rise and go to ring the bell to summon one of the maids. 'We will have tea and then you can tell me all about London.'

Much still troubles me. As Betsy's voice drones on telling of all the wondrous sights she has seen, I ponder this latest information about myself. Lavinia Montgomery. If this tale is true, why should Mr Hawton not have told me? I can understand him being ashamed of his behaviour and hiding me down in Sussex, but why all this secrecy now that we are in Hertfordshire? I am well again, strong in body and mind, why should I care that our families are enemies? Why hide the fact that we eloped? It was romantic as Betsy stated. Why be ashamed of love?

And why does my husband not come to my bed? I shiver at the thought, but in a book I found recently it was written that a good wife must please her husband in all ways. I will do whatever Mr Hawton demands because it is my duty. But he has not tried to take me in his arms; how can he have loved me so much that he arranged to elope with me? There must be more to our story than that which Betsy relates. And why should Mr Hawton care about his mother's feelings? There is no great affection between them—why should he not announce that I am Lavinia Montgomery and he has chosen me to be his wife?

'And so we had tea there, and then Adam saw me onto the Hertford coach and I managed to beg a lift from a carter who was coming to the village this afternoon.' Betsy folds her hands on her lap and smiles complacently.

'Very nice,' I say, not having taken in one word about her adventures. 'I am most grateful for what you have done, Betsy, and you gave Adam the rubies safely?'

'I told you, ma'am.' She opens her eyes

91

wide. 'I've just told you that.'

'Good.' I smile and reach for my sewing. 'Then he will be able to stay on a while longer. I feel that there is still much to be revealed—there are too many unanswered questions.'

'Adam intends seeing that old nurse again in case she remembers something more.'

'I almost feel as if I could confront my husband with the truth,' I say slowly, laying down my work, 'it seems so foolish to go on living a lie now that I know and it is not so dreadful.'

'Oh, I wouldn't do that, ma'am.' Betsy seems upset by the idea. 'Don't say anything yet—not till Adam confirms it.'

'Then there is some doubt?' I watch her closely. 'You have been telling me the truth, Betsy?'

'Of course I have, ma'am. How can you insinuate that Adam and I have been lying? And after all the trouble we've gone to!' She looks most indignant and stands up, about to flounce from the room.

'Betsy dear, don't get angry. I was only voicing a few doubts of my own. Do come and sit down and stop pouting. Don't you understand how muddled I am? I have got to be certain about this, it is my entire life for the first twenty years, or so, and it is very important to me. Please try and understand.'

'Of course I understand, that's why we've both been trying to help you.' She comes back and sits down again but her voice is brittle. 'We are doing all we can, Adam and I, but you don't seem to want to believe us.'

'I do,' I answer wearily, 'but it is a little disconcerting to have a new personage suddenly thrust upon one. I dare say I shall get used to being Lavinia Montgomery in time.'

It had better be all sorted out and confirmed before Christmas, or else with my mother-in-law arriving I shall not know whether to be Lavinia Montgomery, or Miranda Ford. Dear me, what a state to be in. But thoughts of Mother Scurry hearten me; she assured me that a man would come from the south, a man with the answer to all my questions, and I believe her. So all I can do is wait, and once Adam returns I shall know for once and for all who I am, and what befell me a few years ago.

SIX

This evening I cannot sleep. Mr Hawton warned me that he would be late home and not to wait up for him, so Betsy helps me to bed and I snuff out the candle and try to sleep. But too many thoughts struggle in my brain and after hearing the clock strike eleven and then the half-hour, I decide to go downstairs and collect the book which I was reading before Betsy returned. Pulling a wrapper around my shoulders, and taking the candle in my other hand, I creep down the passage to the top of the wide oak staircase. Strange to be so furtive in my own home, I should be able to roam freely, at any hour, where I please. Yet an odd feeling of fear envelops me and I tiptoe carefully down the stairs, starting at every rustle and creak.

As I cross the hall to go to my sitting-room, I see that a light glows through the half-open door of the library. Has Mr Hawton returned, or have the servants forgotten to douse the lights?

Softly I move across to peer round the door and there, slumped in his chair before the dying fire, is my husband. And there is a look of such sorrow on his tired face that my heart turns over. He has always seemed so proud before, so aloof and in control of himself, I have never thought of him having emotions like other people. Anger, yes; strong or fierce feelings, perhaps, but never anything weak like weariness or dejection.

Bella is lying at his feet and at sight of me her tail begins to thump, but she does not attempt to get up.

I stand staring, wondering whether to speak, and as I hesitate Mr Hawton lifts his head and looks towards me. Surprise quickly chases all other emotions from his face, and he is on his feet and coming towards me in an instant.

'What is it, Miranda? Are you all right? Has something happened?'

'No.' I look up into his face, feeling a tenderness which is new to me. 'Why have you not gone to bed? You look weary.'

'I am going now. But what brought you here? Have you a headache?'

I shake my head, my hands clenching at my sides. Now is the time to say it—now!

'I wanted to tell you that I am quite better, that I am prepared to be a good wife, and know—know what a wife should do.' Hot colour floods up from my neck and my cheeks burn. 'If you want to come to my bed, sir, I should not object.'

There! It is said, and I drop my head in shame at having spoken in so open a fashion. But it had to be done—how else can we have a proper marriage?

'Miranda.' His voice is husky and I feel his

hands on my face, lifting my head so that I must look at him. 'Miranda, my dear, you do not know what you say.' For a moment he is silent, looking at my eyes, my hair, my lips, as if he has never seen them before. 'My dear, go up to bed now and do not think about such things again.' His hands drop away and he steps back from me. 'Go on, upstairs with you.'

'You don't love me.' I stare at him in consternation. 'Then why did you marry me? *Why*? You make a mockery of us both and it is not fair!' I am angered by his rejection and do not care if my words hurt him. 'Why do you keep me here like a naughty child, locked away from the outside world? What right have you to deny me my freedom? I want to go out now—want to meet people and make friends. How do you think I feel with only a girl for company, and a husband who is always away in London? I want to laugh and dance and be normal, but you keep me entombed here as if I am an idiot. Why, Mr Hawton, my life is worse than your beloved Bella's!'

I move forward and strike at his chest with my fists. 'You do not love me—you don't show me to your friends or relations—you don't take me about with you. Then let me go! Let me go back to Sussex where I belong.'

'Sussex? What do you know about that?' Mr Hawton grabs hold of my hands and gives me a little shake. 'Who have you been talking to? Why do you mention Sussex? What do you know, Miranda? Tell me.'

This is the old Mr Hawton, the man I know, and once again there is a barrier between us as he gazes down at me with cold eyes.

Bella grunts and rises from her place by the hearth, nosing forward as if she senses that something is amiss.

'I know nothing,' I mutter, 'I have lost my memory and nobody knows anything about me except for my husband, and he is not telling.'

'But why Sussex?' he insists, still holding me fast so that I cannot escape.

'I feel that is where I belong. Your mother mentioned Ladylea and for a moment it seemed that I recognised the name. I can remember nothing more,' I add sulkily, 'but that name is familiar.'

He drops my hands and moves across to the fire to rake over the last of the embers, pushing Bella aside with his foot.

'Be thankful that you know nothing, Miranda. If it were right I would tell you about your past, but I can assure you, my dear, that you are fortunate in having no memory. Do not pry or question, for I warn you that the truth is shocking. Shocking, Miranda—do you hear me?' Mr Hawton straightens and looks across at me with smouldering eyes, a note of violence in his voice. 'So damnable that I would advise you never to question me again. Is that understood?'

I nod, shivering at the sound of his words,

suddenly cold and frightened, wishing that I had not ventured downstairs, that this whole miserable episode had been but one of my nightmares.

'Then go back to your bed,' says my husband harshly, 'and forget everything that has been said tonight.'

Pulling my wrapper more closely around me, I pick up my candle and return to a cold bed and a sleepless night ahead. Betsy has not told me the entire truth. Is she hiding the facts from me? Or has Adam failed to discover what really happened? Dear God, I pray, let Adam come back soon. I must see him and question him myself, he is the only person who can help me now.

*　　　*　　　*

Jake Minns has come. Helen is so happy she never ceases thanking me, and there is a lilt in her voice, a dance in her step, as she moves about the nursery and takes Charlie for his outings. I think they are often at the stables, but Old George has not complained and Helen has a good excuse, for Charlie adores the horses.

I, in turn, try to thank my husband, but our conversations have been stilted since the night I surprised him in the library, and he waves my thanks aside with a brusque gesture.

'One of the lads here was feeling restless

and did not object to going down to Ladylea,' he says curtly. 'So I arranged for him to take Minns' place there.'

I have not seen much of the newcomer for Old George keeps him busy, but one morning I went down to visit Cloud and saw that Helen and Charlie were in the stable yard before me. To my surprise, and annoyance, Jake Minns was holding my son, and as I watched he threw him up in the air high above his head, making the child scream with laughter. Helen was standing by smiling at the spectacle, but there was no sign of Old George.

'What is the meaning of this behaviour?' I moved forward quickly, anger making my voice sharp. 'Take Charlie round to the front gardens at once, Helen, I do not care for such rough play, he is only a babe, after all.'

'Yes, ma'am, beg pardon, ma'am,' and she grabbed my son from the man's powerful arms and scuttled away, very red in the face.

'Have you no work to do?' I stared at Jake Minn's dark, bearded countenance, hating the thought that he had been touching my baby. 'Where is Old George?'

'Gone for tea in the kitchen, ma'am,' he answered gruffly. There was a look in his eyes which discomfited me, a too-familiar, almost insolent expression which vanished as he lowered his head and turned away from me.

'Then carry on with whatever you should be doing in his absence and do not handle my son again, if you please.'

I did not stay to see Cloud and left the stable yard swiftly, with the certain impression that Minns had not returned to his work but was standing, staring after me.

I have spoken to Helen about this incident and she has assured me that she will be more careful with Charlie in future. I am glad that she is happy although I cannot understand her affection for such a lout. It is pleasant to see her obvious contentment, for there is little of that in this house.

Mr Hawton and I have returned to our earlier formal restraint with each other, and Betsy is becoming increasingly awkward. Perhaps her journey to London unsettled her, or the fact that she now knows so much more about me has gone to her head. She is often pert in her behaviour and does not always appear when I ring. Nor is she as constant a companion as once she was, often leaving me alone to go to her room, or down to the village. Perhaps she is in love? Maybe she visits the parson? I do not question her and she does not volunteer information. But her thoughts are often elsewhere, and a smile frequently curves her lips when I can find nothing amusing.

I almost wish that she would leave, but then there would be all the upheaval and bother of engaging a new companion, and in my present disturbed state I could not readily accept a stranger and have to go through explanations all over again.

When Adam comes, I keep telling myself, when he comes back everything will return to normal and we shall be able to settle down to our former contented existence. And perhaps Mr Hawton can be persuaded to give Adam a job on the estate? I miss him; miss his ready laughter and charm. He is the first person I have met with whom I feel quite at ease. My relationship with Betsy was also good, but only to begin with, now it has deteriorated and I doubt whether we shall ever be pleasantly friendly again.

I begin riding more often, sometimes in the mornings as well as in the afternoons, and do not care that Betsy is left on her own. She seems quite happy with her own company and I am glad to be away from her. We ride, Old George and I, farther than I have ridden before but still at a leisurely pace. The exercise and fresh air calm my nerves and it is a pleasure to leave the oppressive atmosphere of the house behind for an hour or so.

When Old George falls sick, Mr Hawton tells Jake Minns to accompany me, and I enjoy our rides together for he is an excellent horseman and does not fear speed. But he is an odd fellow; I cannot understand Helen's fascination for the man, and must admit that I am a little afraid of him. He is so dark, with thick black hair and whiskers, and eyes of so

101

deep a brown that they appear black. Jake Minns has a very striking countenance but there is something about him which repels me, and though he seldom speaks I can feel him watching me, and I am fearful.

*   *   *

Today I realise that it is late November and in a few weeks' time I shall have to play hostess to Mrs Hawton. The thought worries me—how can I entertain her, converse with her, please her? Why do I know so little about the running of a home and how to be a good hostess? Presumably, if part of what Betsy tells is true, I was made to be a recluse like my father, and with my mother dying young I had no one to educate me in matters of etiquette?

As I am finishing breakfast an idea comes to me, and I hurry from the table to find my husband before he goes out.

'I have an idea,' I say, standing firm before the library door so that he cannot get past me. 'Please stay and listen, it is very important.'

Mr Hawton always breakfasts alone, for he is an earlier riser than I, and Betsy is not feeling well this morning so has stayed in her room, thus giving me plenty of time in which to think.

'Yes, Miranda,' he answers in a cool voice, crossing to his chair and sitting down. 'I have ten minutes before meeting Cross. What have you to say?'

I clasp my hands before me and take a deep breath. 'I want to learn to be a proper lady. I do not know where you met me, nor what kind of a life I led before my accident.' Untrue, but there are still doubts in my mind about what Adam has discovered down in Sussex. 'In a few weeks your mother will be coming here to Hazelwood and I have no idea how to manage such a visit. I have read several books about ladies, and how they should run their households, but I need to know much more—I cannot leave everything to Mrs Wanstead, and a good mistress should keep an eye on everything. Would it be possible for you to engage a person who is knowledgeable on the subject, who could teach me to talk and behave in a proper manner?'

Mr Hawton's eyes gleam as I stop speaking, and he seems amused by my outburst. 'I hope you do not imagine that you are inadequate, Miranda? I am most satisfied with you.'

'But I am exactly that, sir. Inadequate!'

'Now, Miranda, who has put such a notion into your head? Has Betsy been upsetting you? I do not think that you and she are as close as you used to be.'

Fancy him noticing that. I always supposed him to be so engrossed in his own thoughts that he did not see what was going on around him.

'Betsy and I get on well enough,' I say

quickly, 'but it is possible to see too much of one person, sir, and as I never go out or meet other people my life is very restricted. Could I not have a teacher and perhaps, once I have learned how to behave properly, we could entertain here? Your mother will think it most strange that we have no friends—you may be able to ignore my questions, but I do not see how you can explain my strange way of life to her!'

Mr Hawton frowns, staring before him at the tips of his polished boots. 'You are right, of course,' he says slowly, 'and now that you are better—fighting fit, in fact,' and he throws me a half-smile, 'I believe your plan to be a good one.' He stands up and collects his gloves and riding-crop from the table. 'Give me a few days to make enquiries, Miranda, but do not change too much. I like you very well as you are.'

'Change can only be for the better, sir. And good for Charlie, too. He is growing up quickly and will soon need play-mates and companions. How can he find friends if his mother is shut away behind closed doors and his father is away in London most of the time?'

Mr Hawton looks at me intently. 'You have also grown up,' he says. 'So much worldly wisdom from one who knows nothing! I do not know whether I have Miss Betsy Potter, or the authors of those books, to thank for the transformation. But I liked you better as you were.'

'I cannot remain shut off from the outside world forever, sir!'

'No, I forgot that you would grow and need to stretch your wings. But do not fly too high, Miranda—you have been hurt once, desperately hurt, I beg you to tread cautiously and not endeavour to know too much.'

'Oh, always these dreadful warnings—these utterings of doom!' I hunch my shoulders and turn from him impatiently. 'I care not what happened before—I want to learn and live now! This is what you have always told me— forget the past and live for the present. So I will, sir! I wish to equip myself with knowledge so that I can live like a normal human being. The past is finished, so do not keep reminding me of it, I beg.'

I swing round and sweep from the room leaving him staring after me.

Well, he deserved that. I am irritated beyond endurance by his mournful looks and dire warnings. If he refuses to tell me what happened then he should keep quiet and not say anything at all. Until Adam returns, I have to try and lead a reasonable life here at Hazelwood, and Mr Hawton's gloomy moods and long face are becoming intolerable. No matter who I was before, as Mrs Hawton of Hazelwood I am *somebody*, and intend improving my mind and manners so as not to feel insignificant when my mother-in-law comes on her Christmas visit.

I also have a duty towards Charlie; never must he be made to feel that his mother is incompetent or stupid. I intend proving to the world that I am an accomplished hostess and a good wife and mother. No one must ever guess at my formidable inadequacies.

My life is improving, part of it, anyway. Twice a week I now drive to Hertford and spend the afternoon with a Miss Clara Hodges. She is an impoverished gentlewoman whose father lost all his money in gambling debts and she now resides, poor soul, in two cramped rooms above a grocer's store. But she lived in a grand house when she was a girl, and she knows all the things I want to hear.

It is such fun travelling into town; I gaze from the carriage windows at the houses and the shops and the people, drinking in all the colour and movement, for I have been starved of civilisation for too long. Old George drives me there, all spruced up in his best uniform, and I alight from the carriage feeling like a lady already.

Miss Hodges's rooms are small and overcrowded with furniture and ornaments, but everything is orderly and clean, and she seems to enjoy my company as much as I do hers. She tells me that she earns a few pence from teaching sewing at the boarding establishment down the road, and she also takes in a few private pupils for elocution lessons. But Miss Hodges's main joy is found in memories of the past, and her pale face glows as we begin our lessons.

'Cards are the first things you must obtain,' she tells me, her voice precise and refined as we sip tea together. 'They are the best means of making acquaintances, and once you begin leaving your card I believe neighbouring ladies will call and do likewise. The cards must be kept in an ivory or gold box, and be engraved with your name in copperplate. Never,' she says firmly, 'never old Gothic script. A lady is a superior being,' she goes on, 'who does no labour and never soils her hands with household tasks.'

'May I arrange flowers?'

I love doing that and should not like to leave such a delicate operation to Mrs Wanstead.

'Flower-arranging is permissible, and needlework,' agrees my companion primly, 'but that is all. Servants are there to serve you and you must never allow familiarity.'

Perhaps that is where I have gone wrong with Betsy, I think, crooking my little finger in the same way as Miss Hodges. We have been too close, too intimate, and she now regards herself as my equal.

And clothing. I have erred there, also.

'Never allow your personal maid to wear flowers in her bonnet, or ribbons in her cap. Long earrings must also be discouraged.

107

Servants must dress plainly to show quite clearly their status in life.'

Not that Betsy is my maid, but she is supposed to serve me, and her choice of attire would not recommend itself to Miss Hodges! In fact, when we visited the cottagers, I believe most of them took Betsy to be the lady of the house. Except for Mother Scurry—she knew who I was before we spoke.

'When you are invited out to luncheon you may remove your fur wrap or cloak, and your gloves, but never take off your bonnet. And do not stay too long. By two-thirty you should be away making social calls.'

Oh, dear, what a lot to remember. I asked Betsy tentatively if she wished to accompany me, thinking that we could discuss the lessons afterwards, but fortunately, as I now realise, she declined. I had hoped to heal the breach between us and felt that this newly acquired knowledge might be useful for her, too, in another position, once she left Hazelwood.

'Another position?' She stared at me when I suggested it. 'I do not intend working like this all my life, ma'am.'

'Then what do you hope to do?' I asked.

'I shall marry a wealthy man. This work here is but a means to an end.'

'Oh.' I was surprised and confused. Parson Andrews could never be called wealthy and Betsy, as his wife, would probably have to work far harder at the vicarage than she did at

Hazelwood. 'Have you any one in mind?' I had not dared to question her before, but now that we were on the subject I felt able to enquire.

'That is my business,' she replied tartly. 'Will you be wanting anything else, or may I go?'

'You may go, Betsy,' I said resignedly. There was little point in keeping her with me when she was in this sullen frame of mind.

So I travel alone to Miss Hodges, driven by Old George, and my companion amuses herself as she pleases during my absence.

We have another letter from Adam. He does not write weekly as he promised, but I suppose there is no point in sending letters if he has nothing new to say. 'Your mother was a beautiful woman, Lady Dreamer,' he writes. The letter was addressed to Betsy, but she hands me the enclosed note and my heart sings at this personal contact from him. 'I have had a further meeting with Annie Malthouse, and seen the little room where you lay during your illness. Annie says that you were a pretty girl before your disfigurement, and your mother was one of the loveliest women she had ever seen. The Montgomerys were friendly with the Hawtons once, a long time ago, and you used to come to children's parties at Ladylea. Then the families quarrelled—Annie does not know the reason—and you never appeared again until that night when Mr Hawton brought you secretly to her cottage.

'You say that there is still a mystery about your past? That your husband speaks of something dreadful happening to you? Annie does not know what this can be, but I think the secret must lie at The Hall. So tomorrow, Lady Dreamer, I am moving my abode nearer to Lewes, and will do my best to brave the Montgomery stronghold. I have told Betsy not to contact me again here—I shall let her know where to write in my next letter. Ever your most humble and devoted slave, Adam.'

Dear Adam. He is the one person who remains steadfast, and my doubts vanish. I feel so strong and confident now, even the worst possible news cannot affect me adversely, though what could have been so tragic is beyond my comprehension. But I know that I can withstand anything, and it will be so pleasant to go to my husband and say—'Look, I know everything now and I do not care. Let us build a new life together, you and me and Charlie.'

And I shall know how to act, and how to control my household; we will give dinner-parties and dances and I shall be a ravishingly beautiful hostess like my mother. And Mr Hawton will be proud of me, he will not go away so much, or better still, he will take me with him and I shall become the toast of London town!

I am happy again and do not fear Christmas, or the fact that my mother-in-law will soon be here. I have a list of menus written out for me by Miss Hodges, and Cook is going to 'have a go', as she puts it, though I rather think that Targets d'Agneau and Paniers d'Orange are beyond her capabilities! Fortunately, Mr Hawton prefers plain cooking, and certainly Cook's roast dinners and fruit tarts are delicious. But for Mrs Hawton we will put on one splendid feast, and I shall write the menu out in French, myself.

I have asked my husband to ascertain whether Miss Somerset will also be coming. I expect she will, and intend preparing two guest chambers, but it will be nice to know in advance. I rather hope she does come—she is a younger lady and not so awe-inspiring as Mr Hawton's mother. She will also be able to help with the conversation, for Betsy will definitely not be present at meal-times.

But what shall I do about my name?

'I told your mother that my name was Miranda Ford before marriage,' I tell my husband that evening. 'She so surprised me by her visit and asked so many questions, I did not know how to answer her.'

'That will do very well,' he replies. 'I have told Mother that you had an unhappy childhood and that she is not to question you about the past.'

'Did you indeed!' He got himself out of trouble very smartly there. 'And I told her that my father was called Samuel and my mother

111

was Margaret, and that we owned a large estate in the north of the county.'

'Really, Miranda,' he says irritably, 'there was no need to embroider the lies. Mother has promised not to pester you—I was quite firm about that.'

'What a pity you were not here to be firm before,' I reply. 'And I also said that I had three brothers and two sisters and that I always spent the New Year with my family. So you'd better take me away somewhere or she'll know that I've been lying.'

'Miranda! You could not have told her so much—you said that you and she only spoke a few words together?' He is on his feet, his brows drawn together in vexation.

'I had time enough,' I say defiantly, enjoying taunting him. 'She was so inquisitive, I had to say something and you had not prepared me for such an inquisition.'

'Mother surely will not stay over until the first of January.' Mr Hawton begins to pace the room.

'It is a long way to come for a mere two or three days, sir.'

He looks up suddenly, warned by the laughter in my voice which I cannot control.

'Are you telling me the truth, Miranda?' Mr Hawton advances on me and catches hold of my shoulders. 'Or are you teasing me?'

'Teasing, sir.'

At the expression on his face I glance down

hastily, surprised by the force of an emotion which I do not recognise. But his hands are warm, burning through the silk of my dress, and he is very close to me and very strong, and I want to swoon but cannot.

He swears then, not loudly but loud enough for me to hear, and shocked, I look up. But his hands have dropped from off my shoulders and he has turned away so that I am unable to see his face.

'Leave me, Miranda,' my husband whispers, and there is an urgency in his voice which frightens me more than his swearing. 'Leave me and get out. Get out, I say!'

I turn and flee from the room, my heart thumping and tears beginning to sting my eyes. What did I do wrong? What happened to us? One minute I am joking with him and for once we have a good and friendly feeling together, then he changes and is now in one of his dark moods, and I am banished like a naughty child to my room.

Betsy is behaving most strangely, too. It is all so provoking, just when I felt that everything was going right for a change.

I was reading late last night and soon after the clock downstairs struck midnight, I heard footsteps outside my door. Knowing that it could not be Mr Hawton, who had retired to his own room over an hour before, I took my candle and moved quickly across to open the door. Holding the candle high I looked down the corridor and saw Betsy disappearing into her chamber.

Angry and perturbed I hurried down the passage and flung open the door.

'Where have you been?'

She turned, her face white as death in the candle-light, her pale eyes icy. 'That is none of your business and you have no right to come barging in here without knocking!'

'I have every right to know what my servant is doing creeping around the house past midnight. Where were you, Betsy—answer me, or I shall call Mr Hawton.'

'I would not do that if I were you, ma'am.' There was a snarl in her voice and her enmity startled me. 'I have been out but I am now back here in my room and wish to sleep. Kindly leave me alone.' She stood very still before me, and there was mud on her shoes and on the hem of her gown. 'Call your husband, if you dare, ma'am, but I would not advise it. I really would not advise you to do such a foolish thing.' And she smiled, without mirth, her eyes daring me to act.

'Very well, Betsy, I shall not waken him. But we must have words in the morning. I really think it would be best if you left Hazelwood. Neither you nor I are benefiting from your employment here and it would be better if you went back home.'

She raised her eyebrows. 'Hoity-toity, ma'am, don't speak in that fashion to me. You forget that I know a great deal about you now, and I do not think that Mr Hawton would like it if I voiced my knowledge abroad. And I can tell people much—much more than you realise.' There was a sneer in her voice and her eyes glittered with malice. 'Don't worry, ma'am, I fully intend leaving Hazelwood—but I shall go when it suits me, and not when *you* desire it.'

I stood speechless, not knowing what to say, aghast at the hostility which she no longer troubled to hide.

'You were kind once, Betsy,' I said at last. 'You cared about people, about the cottagers, and we had fun together. What has happened to change you?'

'Kind? Yes, I wanted to help *them* because they lived as I have done—I know all about their filth and poverty—I was brought up the same way myself. But you!' She spat out the words. 'You are everything I hate and despise—moaning away here about your lost memory—squalling and weeping because you cannot remember. Pah! I wish that I could not remember. Would like to claw all memory from my brain! But you have everything that money can buy, Mrs High and Mighty Hawton, you are spoilt and pampered with your fine house and beautiful clothes, your wealthy husband and carriages and horses. You don't deserve them, you don't. So go back to your lonely bed and leave me be. And next time you hear footsteps outside your door, don't bother to investigate. You won't get any humble confessions from me! I go where I like and do as I please, and you no longer control me, thank God!'

She moved swiftly, pushing me backwards out of her room, shutting the door so quickly that the draught blew out my candle and I had to feel my way back to my room in inky darkness.

SEVEN

It is the twenty-third of December. Tomorrow our visitors arrive and I am looking forward to their coming. Mr Hawton has been away so much this autumn that I welcome the chance to have him here, and this house is so big it will be pleasant to hear voices and have all the hustle and bustle of guests. It will be good for the servants, also. They have become slack of late with the master so seldom at home, and now that Betsy and I no longer take our meals together, I have begun sitting in my little parlour with my meal set before me on a low table by my knee. I do not know if Betsy bothers about food, whether she eats in her room, or with Mrs Wanstead. But I doubt the latter for she and the housekeeper have never been friendly. Maybe she takes bread and cheese from the kitchen and that suffices. The only times I see her now are in the mornings, early, to help me dress; at night before going to bed, and also at tea time. I have insisted upon this, for she is engaged to be my companion and the other servants must see us together at intervals, or else word might reach my husband's ears and he would be very angry. When Mr Hawton is at Hazelwood Betsy still joins us at meal times, so we keep up a semblance of normality; but it is a great strain on me and I long more than ever for Adam's return. He might be able to talk some sense into Betsy, or at least explain her extraordinary attitude to me.

Early this month I did as Miss Hodges suggested and called at three nearby estates, leaving my card. But only one lady returned my call, a Mrs Cavendish, and she was so prim and proper, looking down her nose at me, that I was thankful when she took her leave.

Mrs Cavendish had two young daughters who were in the charge of a governess, she informed me, and her son went to Eton. At first I did not know what she meant by that name.

'Eton?' I queried, feeling my hands become sticky with perspiration, realising that this tea-time chat was going to be more difficult than I had anticipated.

'Yes, yes,' returned the lady impatiently, 'that fine public school. Where does Mr Hawton intend educating his son?'

'Parson Andrews is supervising the building of a school in the village—' I began.

'The village school!' My companion looked shocked. 'That won't do—won't do at all, my dear Mrs Hawton. Your son must be educated privately.'

Privately? Just now she had mentioned a public school—it was most confusing.

'Perhaps a tutor?' I said diffidently.

Charlie was still a baby and his schooling a

far distant affair, but I certainly had no intention of sending him away from Hazelwood. How wicked to separate a little boy from his family.

'A tutor is not the thing at all unless the child is mentally backward.' Mrs Cavendish stared at me with suspicion. 'Have you any cause to doubt his mental abilities?'

'No, indeed not!' I might have lost my memory but Charlie was sound in both mind and limb. The audacity of the woman! 'I simply find the idea of sending him away from home quite repugnant. Were you not sad when your son went away?'

'No. I knew that he would be receiving a first-class education and mixing with the best people. There are too many females in our household and Mr Cavendish wanted Arthur to grow up a man, away from our frills and petticoats. You must not spoil your boy, Mrs Hawton, he must learn to rough and tumble with other lads and stand on his own feet.'

She was doubtless glad to be rid of him—a less maternal female I could not imagine, with her sharp features and thin neck and pale protuberant eyes.

'Do you have an establishment in London, Mrs Hawton?' my companion continued relentlessly. 'For then you could drive over to Windsor and visit your son on occasion.'

'Er, no. But my husband is often in town and is looking for a suitable house for us.'

119

'Very wise.' She nodded. 'We spend part of every winter there, entertaining and going to the opera. Of course the girls are too young to accompany us at present, but it will be part of their education later on, and then we will go for the London Season and find suitable husbands for them.'

'Of course,' I smiled.

'I expect you will be adding to your family before long and then you will have the worries I now have. Dear me, a son is a joy, but the girls are a constant problem and will continue to plague me until they are off my hands.'

'What a pity that you cannot send them away to school,' I remarked.

'And waste all that money? What are you thinking of, Mrs Hawton? Ah, I see that was meant as a joke.' She sniffed, unamused. 'Girls do not need to know anything apart from needlework and music, and perhaps a little French.'

'Yes, indeed.' Her presence was becoming tedious and I wished that she would take her leave and go.

'You do not entertain much, Mrs Hawton? For how long have you resided at Hazelwood? I got the shock of my life when I saw your card. Fancy her calling, I said to Lady Millwood, we had quite decided that you were a recluse!'

'I have been here for nearly two years but have suffered from ill-health,' I explained quickly. 'It is only of late that I have felt able to receive callers.'

'You are not from this part of the country? I did not see the announcement of your wedding in the newspaper, but my husband knows Mr Hawton and he says that you are from Sussex.'

'Yes, from near the town of Lewes.' Would she never cease prying and go? It was not a good idea to leave cards around the neighbourhood—at least, not until I knew more about my past. And what did Mr Hawton want me to say? How was I supposed to answer such questions?

'That's a pretty gown. Might I be so bold as to ask who made it?'

'Miss Ostrey.'

Mrs Cavendish looked blank. 'Miss Ostrey? Is she in Bond Street? I have an excellent milliner there called Dacre—but I have not heard of Ostrey.'

'She is a seamstress in the village and is most obliging and comes up whenever I want her,' I replied.

'From the village? Dear me, that isn't the thing at all.' My companion's sharp nose twitched in dismay. 'I mean, the material is pretty enough, but one can see that the garment was not finished by accomplished hands. Let me give you the address, Mrs Hawton, and next time you are in town be sure and visit Miss Dacre. Her bonnets are a delight and there is an excellent gownshop

121

next door. Mention my name and remember number seventy, Bond Street. Have you got that?'

'Thank you,' I said weakly. 'Will you have more tea, ma'am?'

'No, indeed,' she answered, to my great relief, 'we have a dinner engagement this evening and I must be returning home to prepare myself.'

Once my visitor departed, I went to my little sitting-room and sat down, quite exhausted.

It is all Mr Hawton's fault. If he were at home more, taking an interest in local events, getting to know the neighbouring gentry, taking me out driving so that we become known in the district, everything would be better and life more cheerful. But he spends more time in London than he does at home, and I spend my time avoiding Betsy and reading, sewing and riding. Hazelwood resembles a house of the dead more than a happy family home. And when I do make the effort to meet people, my lack of knowledge lets me down. Miss Hodges's information is all very well, but I need to know so much more than she can teach me. I need to know about *myself*, and become a complete person before endeavouring to entertain inquisitive females!

Thank God for Charlie. He is an enchanting little boy and helps to take my mind off my loneliness, but I shall never allow him to go away to school. Soon he will be needing playmates; his first birthday party was attended by me and Helen, with Mrs Wanstead and the maids coming up with their small gifts at the end of the afternoon. Betsy did not put in an appearance, but that did not disturb me. She has seen so little of Charlie lately that I think, and hope, that he has forgotten her.

Even Mr Hawton did not return in time for his son's birthday, but he seemed apologetic when I informed him of the fact, and has since given the child a splendid set of tin soldiers, which are far too advanced for him at present, but which he will doubtless appreciate in time.

Next year I am quite determined that Charlie shall have a proper party. And if by then I still cannot cope with the ladies of the district, I shall turn to the village. Charlie is going to have friends whether they are well born, or not. I shall call on the doctor's wife and ask her assistance, and open the house to the butcher, the baker, and the candlestick-maker! They, at least, will not question me about my past. My mother-in-law would not approve but she will not be here at that time of year, and my son is not going to grow up like me, shut away from the world.

But enough of the future. Miss Ostrey has made me a new gown of rose-pink taffeta and I shall wear it on Christmas Day. Pink is a colour which suits Miss Somerset, she wore that hue the first time I saw her. But I do not look badly in it, and with my hair longer now and caught behind my ears, and wearing the pearls which my husband gave me the last time he came back from London, I should pass well enough.

There is still an hour to dinner. Mr Hawton is closeted in the library which, like my sitting-room, is his private place where he does not like being disturbed. Betsy is, as usual, away in her room and as there is time to spare I decide to try on my new gown.

Betsy will have to help me on Christmas Day, but it does not matter that the buttons are not properly done up tonight, and I pull and smooth the rich, rustling material, admiring my reflection in the mirror. My waist appears tiny above the full skirts, and my shoulders gleam white in the candlelight.

Very pretty, Lavinia. Laughing, I lean forward and kiss my face in the glass.

Foolish girl! I stare, enchanted by my image, and pinch my cheeks so that they glow as pink as my dress. Then I lift out the pearls from their black velvet nest in the jeweller's box and hold them to my throat. They gleam, soft and translucent against my skin, and I hope that my husband will be proud of me. There is certainly nothing to be ashamed of in my appearance; I have pulled several small curls forward across my brow to hide the scar, which is gradually beginning to fade, thank goodness, and my eyes are luminous and happy as they look back at me.

But Miss Somerset is very pretty, also. And plumper than I am—perhaps I am too thin? My bosom is small and my arms slender, maybe I would not be very comfortable to cuddle? I think of Miss Somerset's rounded body and imagine it suddenly without clothes on. Then, blushing, I turn from my reflection and put the pearls back in their box.

Be brave, I chide myself, you are tall and elegant, and dressed like this there is nothing with which your mother-in-law or your husband can possibly find fault. And you are Lavinia Montgomery, as well bred as the Cavendishes or the Somersets, and you can take your place next to the best of them.

It has been decided by my husband that I shall continue the masquerade of being Miranda Ford, and he is convinced that his mother will not question me. But deep inside I know that I am really Lavinia, and it pleases me to think that I shall be fooling both Mrs Hawton and her son.

Stepping back in a careless dancing movement, I tread upon my gown, which has not been properly fastened, and the heel of my shoe catches in the material. There is a sickening, wrenching sound, and when I pull the skirt round to examine the damage I see a long rent in the taffeta. Thank heavens there is time to mend the tear. I struggle out of the garment, throw my wrapper over my petticoats and the dress over my arm, and hurry down the passage to Betsy's room. Whether she likes it or not, this is a chore which she must do for me; in twenty minutes I must go downstairs to join Mr Hawton for the evening meal, and tomorrow our guests arrive.

I knock briskly but there is no answer. Perhaps she has gone out? I knock again, then hear a scuffling sound before the door is opened a crack.

'Oh, it's you,' Betsy says, 'come in.' And she flings the door open wide. Her hair is loose about her shoulders, and she wears nothing but her chemise, and her feet are bare.

Then I see Adam, *Adam*, half-reclining on her bed, his jacket off and his hair rumpled.

'Good-evening, Lady Dreamer.' He smiles across at me. 'How very nice to see you again.'

For a moment faintness envelops me and I sag against the door which Betsy has shut behind me.

'You!'

'Get some smelling-salts,' Adam orders. 'We don't want the lady collapsing on us, do we?'

'What are you doing here? Why did you not tell me you were coming?' I whisper, staring at his amused face; the same bright blue eyes, the same wide curving mouth.

'But I am often here, Lady Dreamer, this visit is not remarkable. It is only that you have not seen me here before. Wake up, dear lady, wake up to the facts. Betsy, the salts!'

She shoves a bottle beneath my nose but I

126

knock it away with my hand, anger sweeping over me, giving me strength.

'When did you get back from Sussex?'

Adam leans against the pillow, folding his hands behind his head, stretching out his legs. 'Sussex? I have never been to Sussex.'

I gasp and Betsy draws up a chair and pushes me on to it. 'Sit down,' she says, 'I don't intend picking you up off the floor.'

'But you went to Sussex, to Ladylea, and found out about my past and met Annie—'

I break off as he shakes his head, his mouth pulled down in mock sorrow.

'No, no, I never travelled any further than Hertford. We made up those letters, Betsy and I. But we did add some interest to your life, you must admit that, Lady Dreamer.'

'Don't call me that!' I cannot bear the caressing way in which he utters that damned name. 'You mean that it was all lies? There is no Lavinia Montgomery? All that tale about my father, and me eloping with Mr Hawton, and—'

'All lies,' he says, shaking his head, 'all lies, I'm afraid.'

'But we had great fun making it all up,' adds Betsy, with a giggle. 'I thought of the climbing out of the window bit, and Adam made up the name and all that about your poor old father. I wanted Daphne, myself, but Adam said Lavinia sounded more elegant.'

'Shut your mouth!' I turn on her with such

127

venom that she blanches and shrinks away.

'Don't you shout at me.' She clambers on to the bed and sits, swinging her legs defiantly. 'You are nothing except ignorant and I'm glad we've hurt you.'

'But why?' I appeal to Adam. 'Why do this to me? Why pretend?'

'We needed money and it did not seem right that you had so much and we had nothing. So Betsy and I devised this little plan and it worked. We are to marry soon—I have almost enough saved and then you will not be bothered by our presence any longer.'

'Money saved?' Then it came to me. Stupidly I had not thought of it before. 'My jewels! You have sold them and used the money for your own purpose? How *could* you be so wicked, and you, a parson's son! Oh, I cannot believe it of you, I cannot!'

'Parson's son, or not, I must live and you must admit that you have more than enough, my dear Mrs Hawton. You cannot really miss that frippery, and Betsy tells me that your loving spouse has but recently given you more. Pearls, I believe? Betsy and I want to set up house, we want our own home, and you will know that you have helped us in our aim. A most charitable action, dear lady.'

'How dare you? How dare you lounge there and tell me all this—have you no sense of shame? Wait till I tell my husband.' I stand up and head for the door. 'I shall tell Mr Hawton

128

this moment about the pair of you and he'll soon wipe that smile off your handsome, cheating face!'

Betsy jumps from her perch on the bed and runs to bar my way. 'You won't tell your husband anything,' she says softly, crouching before me like a cat about to spring.

'I shall. Get out of my way!'

'Mrs Hawton,' Adam calls behind me, 'if you say one word to your husband I shall tell him that you are my mistress, that we have spent many pleasurable hours together in bed.'

I spin round, aghast at his intention. 'What do you mean? The idea is preposterous. Mr Hawton would never believe you!'

'Would he not?' Adam swings his legs to the floor and stands, yawning in a leisurely fashion. 'I would say that you gave me those jewels, ma'am, in payment for my—er—personal services, your husband being somewhat tardy in such matters. And Betsy would back me up. I know certain things about your body, ma'am, that only a lover could know.'

I blush to the roots of my hair as Betsy titters behind me. I have a birthmark, a red patch high on my right leg, which only she can have told him about.

'You would not dare!'

'I certainly would.' He nods gravely. 'And I also have in my possession a letter, written by you, calling me "dearest Adam", thanking me

129

for all that I have done for you, saying that you hope to see me again very soon, that I have made you happy. Those words are written for all to see in your own hand, dear lady. I think your husband would believe me, you know.'

Oh, God! I had written that, and the meaning could be misconstrued. How could Adam be so vicious—so wicked?

'You are a thief and a liar,' I spit, hatred raging in my breast, wanting to tear at his handsome face with my nails, claw out his eyes with my trembling fingers.

'Now, now, not a thief,' he says, 'you gave me those gems, ma'am, of your own free will. Remember? And who knows if I have lied? Perhaps what I said was true. You cannot call me a liar until you have proved me wrong.'

I close my eyes, wondering where to turn, what to do; that these two can have behaved so shamelessly towards me is still hard to accept. But they are here, in this room. I open my eyes to see Betsy, dishevelled and voluptuous in her near nakedness, and Adam—the man I had trusted, the one person whom I had believed would set my shaky world to rights; Adam, handsome, honest-eyed and charming; Adam, to behave in such a wicked fashion. Oh, it was not to be endured.

'When will you go?' I whisper. 'When will you leave me in peace?'

'When we are ready.' Betsy puts up a hand and touches her hair. 'Adam must stay a while with Mrs Norton, then we shall disappear.'

'Mrs Norton?'

'She is a wealthy widow in Hertford with whom Adam has been living. Looks upon him as her son, doesn't she, Adam? And he takes great care of her. Nearly blind, she is, and housebound and a bit queer in the head. But she has taken to him and he cannot leave her yet.'

'Does he steal from her, also?' My voice cracks with contempt.

'What the eye doesn't see,' Adam says, and winks. 'She has no children and it would be a pity if all that wealth went to waste. She spoils me, ma'am, and I am very grateful, very attentive. It is tiring work, requiring considerable patience, but we are winning.' And he looks across at Betsy and laughs.

'It won't be long,' Betsy assures me, her eyes pale and cruel in her white face. 'We won't stay longer than we have to, do not fear. But remember, ma'am, not one word to your husband or you will rue it. Tell him that I am indisposed and therefore will not be dining with you tonight.'

I return her look in silence, then she steps to one side and allows me to leave. As I begin to walk down the corridor, my legs like jelly, scarce holding me up, she calls after me.

'Oh, ma'am, I think you have forgotten something.'

On to the floor at my feet she hurls the

rose-pink taffeta gown.

*   *   *

We are gathered in the drawing-room, Mrs
Hawton, Miss Somerset, my husband and I,
after dinner and my mother-in-law even deigns
to offer her congratulations on the fare. It was
Cook's normal, everyday type of food—roast
and fruit tart—with which she copes well, and
I know that our Christmas dinner will be
equally good. But it is the new-fangled French
menu which will flummox her and I have my
doubts about Saturday's repast. However, food
is the last thing on my mind at present; I feel
slightly sick and my head is beginning to throb.

It was a strain greeting my mother-in-law on
her arrival here, as if I had not a care in the
world, listening to her with the undivided
attention of a good hostess, smiling at Miss
Somerset and playing the part of a charming
and accomplished wife. A terrible strain, whilst
all the time my mind was roving to last night
and the appalling scene with Adam. I kept
hearing Betsy's voice, her mocking laughter. 'I
wanted Daphne but Adam chose Lavinia—it
sounded more elegant.'

I have been abruptly thrown back into the
abyss of despair—of nothingness, yet it seems
worse now than it did before. They have taken
away hope, torn my little world apart and
thrown the pieces to the ground and trampled

132

upon them with careless laughter.

'Such a darling boy,' Miss Somerset is saying now, slanting her blue eyes at my husband, 'and grown so much since we last saw him. You must be extremely proud of your son, Robert.'

Robert. I have never called him that.

'I am proud, indeed.' My husband glances at me, wondering why I am so quiet.

But I have given all that I can give, have laughed and talked and been as gracious as possible during the past few hours. Now I have relapsed into silence, longing to leave the room, get away from them all, seek the sanctuary of my bedchamber.

'You must be thinking of more children soon.' Mrs Hawton's eyes are fixed upon my waist as she fingers the amethysts on her breast. 'You must have a large family, Robert. This house is too empty. And I know, for I have never got over Simon's death. Provide for the future, Robert, no one can tell what may happen in life and I desire a great many grandchildren.' She is wearing a lilac-coloured gown which does not become her; her skin is too sallow and her great dark eyes are not enhanced by such an insipid shade. 'Of course, Miranda comes from a large family,' she goes on, 'she must miss her brothers and sisters. Do they often visit, dear?'

My husband shifts in his chair as I stare at him for support.

'Not often as yet. I told you that Miranda

133

has been ill, Mother, and has had to lead a very quiet life until now.'

'Poor dear, I remember she was unwell the last time we saw her.' She finds my state of health tiresome and it shows in her voice.

'Miranda enjoys riding,' says my husband, changing the subject. 'Minns has settled down well and Old George is pleased with him. I trust that the lad I sent in exchange is proving satisfactory?'

My mother-in-law nods but is intent upon turning the conversation back to me. 'What exquisite pearls, dear, I meant to remark on them earlier. A peace token, no doubt, after one of Robert's frequent trips to London?'

'Yes.' I am so tired that I can hardly keep my eyes open. How soon can I make an escape? Would it be impolite to leave now? To remain much longer in this stifling room and withstand more questioning will be intolerable.

'You are too often in town, Robert,' admonishes his mother. 'Mr Wheeler says he frequently sees you at the club. Now that you have a young family I really think you should curtail your former extravagances and settle down as a country squire, with your nice little wife.'

Mr Hawton stands up and moves to place another log upon the fire which is already burning brightly, causing my head to buzz from the heat. Betsy has also laced me uncomfortably tightly, and what with the wine

134

at dinner to which I am unaccustomed, and now the heat of the room, I am feeling dizzy as well as fatigued. But I cannot faint again in Mrs Hawton's presence, she will think me a fearfully weak creature if I do.

I fix my eyes upon Miss Somerset, who is chattering brightly, and try to concentrate on what she is saying.

'It was a lovely evening.' She is freshly pretty in primrose yellow silk, with lace at her wrists and shoulders. 'You remember the Latimers, don't you, Robert? They were asking after you—it is so long since they saw you. They could not believe it when I said that you had at last settled down with a wife and baby son.'

'I remember them.' He *has* seated himself again but is looking at me and there is concern on his face. 'Perhaps we should all retire early,' he says. 'You must both be tired after your journey and tomorrow will be a busy day.'

'Did you give Miranda the rubies?' I hear my mother-in-law's voice ring out with awful clarity. 'The Hawton rubies, Robert, which traditionally go to the eldest son's bride. Of course, Simon had them, but no doubt they were passed on to you.'

Mr Hawton smiles, and as he looks across at me I clutch at the arm-rests of my chair, my body rigid, seeing his face through a blood-coloured haze.

'Yes, Mother, I gave them to Miranda as a wedding present. You must wear them tomorrow, my dear, they will look splendid with your new gown.'

All the panic of the last days engulfs me, and with a sudden burst of horror I stand, clutching at my head with my fists, and I see their astonished faces and foolish open mouths as I scream.

I scream over and over again as Mr Hawton rushes to me, and his mother falls back in consternation on the sofa, and Miss Somerset runs to ring the bell. I am still screaming as they carry me upstairs to my bedroom, and it is only after Betsy undresses me and bundles me into bed with a warming-pan at my feet, that my cries turn to moans and then to whispered sobs. She makes me drink some water with some of Dr Ingram's powders and then I am aware of my husband tiptoeing into the room and bending over me.

'Go to sleep now, Miranda,' he says huskily. 'I'll see you in the morning. Forgive me, my dear, for putting you through such an ordeal, I had not realised what a strain it would be for you.'

Then he tells Betsy to leave me and they go out together allowing me to sink into oblivion.

EIGHT

Mr Hawton is my constant companion after that night, coming to sit with me every morning and afternoon. He talks, telling me of his past, remembering childhood incidents and youthful escapades. Sometimes I listen and sometimes his voice is but a blurred monotone, as thoughts chase round and round in my brain. What is going to happen to me? How can I explain the loss of those jewels? What point is there in leaving my bed and trying to live again?

I suppose my husband cares, else why should he sit by me for hour after hour? But it was earlier this year that I needed him, before Betsy and I became so intimate. Why did he not ride with me, take me about with him, talk to me then? Now it is too late. Betsy and Adam have planned too well and I am trapped.

As Mr Hawton's voice drones on I think and ponder and try to plan. Mother Scurry—could she help me? Dare I put my trust in another human being?

Betsy is still here. She moves softly about the room and administers to my needs, but she never stays long, thank God, and does not speak. She must be able to feel my hatred it is so intense. But she is very quiet, very contained; no doubt it suits her to remain here for the present, and she must feel quite safe knowing that I dare not tell about her and Adam.

Adam! Does he still creep to her bed at night? Do they kiss and cuddle in the darkness, laughing at their cleverness, whilst I lie drugged and inert but a few doors down the passage?

Helen brings Charlie down to see me every afternoon and he does not appear to find it strange that his mama is silent, lying in her bed. He is a bundle of energy and always manages to stir me from my lethargy, as I hold him to my breast for the short time that he will allow the embrace. I smell the clean baby smell of him and feel his rounded limbs and stroke his soft hair. He is pure and good and wholesome, something to cling to, the only being untouched by wickedness or deceit.

Even my husband must confess to me although I do not wish to hear.

'I had a wild youth, Miranda,' he says, as I turn my face to the wall, wishing that he would go away and spare me his guilt. 'Simon tended to lead me astray; I was several years younger and it amused him to teach me the ways of the world, so that I became spoilt and very head-strong. I hope that you will forgive me my past for you will doubtless hear rumours, and my mother was right about what she called my "extravagances".' He sighs and leans forward

138

to take my hand. 'I should not have married you, my dear, but have tried to make amends and hope that one day you will understand. Now, however, I intend remaining here at Hazelwood. You will become strong again and we will spend more time together. Let us start afresh, Miranda, and when you are quite well I shall endeavour to be a better husband. We will entertain, as you once desired, and we will invite people to our home and build a happy family life for Charlie. What say you to that?'

I remain silent—for if he needs forgiveness what about me? How can I ever explain about the rubies, and the other missing gems? And he has said nothing about my past. Mr Hawton may talk about his childhood or not, as it pleases him, but what about mine? How can we ever have a good life together if he refuses to tell me about myself? I have had my fill of dishonesty, and if my husband cannot be open with me there will be no hope of the happy family life he wishes to achieve.

Mother Scurry. Every day I think about her and believe that she is the answer to my needs; an old woman with a black hat and a bundle of weeds, perhaps, but also a being of wisdom and power. She was wrong about Adam, though. Her 'man from the south' told me nothing but a pack of lies. Can she possibly aid me further? Yet if I do not seek her help there is no one else to whom I can go.

Gradually strength returns and with it the

knowledge that I must act soon; Mr Hawton will be wanting me up and about, playing hostess to his guests, wearing my expensive gowns and jewels, and I must know what to do before my foolhardy act is discovered. For if he finds out about the rubies before Betsy leaves she will think that I have told my husband, and she and Adam will relate their dreadful tale and Mr Hawton will believe them. Then what will become of me? He might take Charlie away from me; say that I am a faithless wife, unfit to be a mother. He might divorce me—what would I do then? At least I am safe here at Hazelwood, protected and cared for. But if I were thrown out to fend for myself—a woman without a husband to shield her, with no memory—dear God, I should die.

*   *   *

My chance comes when Mr Hawton is out one morning. Parson Andrews arrives to discuss the new school and then my husband goes with him to inspect the building. I am sitting in my parlour attempting some tapestry, although my heart is not in the intricate work, when Mr Hawton comes in to tell me that he will be away for an hour or so. I nod, keeping my face expressionless. I must get out the moment they leave.

To Mrs Wanstead I say that I am going out

for a breath of fresh air. Betsy and I have been taking short outings in the garden, when the weather has been clement, so that my strength has returned and I feel at last able to walk the distance to Mother Scurry's cottage. Of late Betsy has been with me more; with Mr Hawton constantly at home she has had to act the part of companion, even though such proximity has been painful to us both. But this morning she has gone down to arrange flowers in the church, providing me with the opportunity to go where I wish without being observed.

As I pass the stables, Jake Minns is cleaning out one of the stalls, and he turns as I go quickly by, and stares after me. I can feel his watchful eyes upon me until there is a bend in the lane, and the back of my neck prickles at the intensity of his gaze. Doubtless he has heard about my indisposition and is pleased to see me up and about again, but I do not feel easy until I am well down the lane and out of sight of the house and stables.

It is with a feeling of greater relief that I eventually cross the field and head for Mother Scurry's cottage. I am not as strong as I thought—with Betsy I have never strolled for more than ten minutes at a time—and my body is trembling with weariness as I lift my hand to knock. It will be pleasant to sit down for a while and perhaps be offered more of her dandelion tea.

The door opens a crack and her familiar wrinkled face peers out. On seeing me she opens the door wide and pulls me roughly inside.

'I have been waiting, mistress,' she says, hoarsely, 'you have been a long time coming. But where is the child? Have you not spoken to Jake Minns?'

I pull back from her fierce grip; she is different this time, less suppliant, more aggressive.

'Jake Minns? I do not understand. Why should I speak to him? And why did you expect Charlie? This is not the sort of place to which I would bring a baby.' I speak coldly, disliking her avaricious stare. It was a mistake to come—this old harridan cannot help me.

Hastily Mother Scurry touches my arm but lightly now, a gentle caress. 'There now, mistress, don't take on so. Sit yourself down and rest for I can see that you are weary.' She pulls forward a chair, smiling her toothless smile. 'Perhaps I was wrong, but I sensed an urgency, a need for help, and thought you had escaped here to safety with your boy.'

She tugs at my hand and I sit, my legs shaky and unwilling to hold me up a minute longer.

'I am in need of advice and seek your aid, Mother Scurry, but it is only for me. Why should Charlie be in need of assistance? He is not involved in this miserable affair.' I stare at her bent form as she shuffles round to the fire and busies herself with the kettle of water. 'And what of Jake Minns? Why did you mention his name? Do you know him?'

'He holds the key to all your problems, mistress, you must speak to him alone. He comes from Ladylea, does he not? And knows about your past. I told him to speak to you.' Vexation sounds in her voice, then she sighs and turns to offer me a cup of tea. 'There—I must not be impatient—the time will come. Drink this, mistress, it will give you strength.'

'The man from the south!' I take the cup, my eyes fixed upon her wrinkled face. 'You told me about him and I thought you meant Adam. But it was Jake Minns all the time, and I have sensed that he was interested in me—he keeps watching.' I shiver. 'I do not like the man, Mother, how can he help me?'

'He knows. You see, he was there.' Her wizened face is full of certainty. 'He must tell you everything before you come again, and when you do, let no one know of it, mistress, else I cannot help you.' She leans forward, peering at me intently from beneath her black hat. 'You have not spoken of me to your husband? Nobody knows that you visit here? Nobody saw you come today?'

I shake my head and begin to sip the hot brew. 'I have told no one. But Jake Minns saw me when I passed the stables, he may have guessed where I was heading.'

'He does not matter—you may confide in

him. We understand each other and he has the gift, also. Have you seen him with the horses, whispering in their ears? Aye, he has a way with him, and wisdom, he is a whisperer, child, and can make those beasts do anything he wants.'

'A whisperer?' Once again my skin quivers in fear. 'I know he is good at his work, but Bella does not like him.'

'Bella?' The old woman lifts her head with a jerk.

'Mr Hawton's dog.'

She grunts. 'Dogs know. They are clumsy beasts—I have no time for them, but they can be a nuisance. You do not take her about with you—she has not followed you here?'

'Bella only goes with my husband and I do not like her, either.' The rest and warm drink have revived me and I sit forward, wanting to bring my troubles to the old woman's attention. 'Mother Scurry, what am I to do? I was stupid enough to give away some valuable jewellery which my husband gave me, and now he and his mother are talking about the gems and I will be expected to wear them and—'

'The jewels do not matter,' she breaks in, 'I have told you that once you have heard what Jake Minns has to say those rubies will become unimportant. Do not fret so, mistress. You have only to learn the secret of your past and then come to me. Once you are safely here again all your problems will be solved.'

'How do I know that I can trust you? I have already put my trust in someone and been most cruelly used.' I bite my lip, remembering Adam's honest eyes and beguiling smile.

'You cannot know. But I am asking nothing from you, mistress, neither gold nor silver. You have nothing to lose by trusting in me. All I ask is that you speak to Jake Minns and after that everything will become clear to you and you will know exactly what to do. Go back now but do not attempt to see the man today. Go to him tomorrow morning, when you are refreshed after a night's sleep, then come to me in darkness. Do not risk another visit in daylight. If anybody should see you with me, or guess your intent, I would be unable to assist you.'

I stand, drawing my shawl tightly around my body. 'Is the truth very dreadful?'

She looks at me in silence, her eyes gazing through me, or so it seems. 'It is bad,' she says finally, 'but 'tis better than the unknown. I do not think that you can go on for much longer as you are.'

'That is true.' I turn towards the door. 'And Charlie?' I look back at her. 'Charlie is involved in all this?'

'Go, go!' she cries, angry again. 'I cannot answer all these questions, the man must do that. Go and see him and then come back to me.'

She is a witch, that much is certain, but the knowledge does not frighten me. I am conscious of her powers, yet unafraid. But a whisperer! The word strikes cold in my heart and its sinister ring suits the man's dark countenance. But how can Jake Minns, a man gifted with horses, know about me? I did not even know how to ride before coming to Hazelwood. Useless to ponder, somehow, some time tomorrow, I must see him on his own and get him to tell me everything. I shudder at the thought, apprehensive at having to spend time in the man's company, realising with panic that Lavinia Montgomery is no more. She was a safe, normal sort of person with whom I could identify, and her tale was not frightening; I could believe in her without fear. But my husband warned me that my past was shocking, and now I shall have to summon up all my courage to accept the truth from a stranger who repulses me. And this time, I believe, it will really be the truth.

Next morning I announce that I feel fit enough to ride again, and when Mr Hawton says that he will accompany me I have to quickly think of an excuse.

'Let this first time be with Old George, or Jake Minns,' I say. 'I wish to surprise you with my prowess and it is a long time since I last rode Cloud. Allow me to have a practice first,

146

sir.' I smile sweetly, willing him to agree. 'I would not want you to be disappointed in me—we have never ridden together, have we? So today I wish to go out with one of the grooms, just for a short spell, and then I shall be ready for you and we shall have a proper ride.'

'Very well.' He does not appear put out by my childish request, indeed, it seems to amuse him. 'Have your dress rehearsal, Miranda, and tomorrow we will ride together as you suggest.'

'Will it be all right if I ask for Jake Minns to accompany me? May I tell Old George that you ordered it? I find the old man so grumpy at times—his manner depresses me.'

'So long as you do not go out alone I care not which of the grooms goes with you. Minns is an excellent horseman, ask for him by all means, and if Old George turns cantankerous refer him to me.'

It is a beautiful crisp morning, the frost glistening white upon the grass as we canter across the park. I feel calm after my night's sleep and able to cope with anything. So be it, I think. Let us get this matter resolved for once and for all, then when the grim truth is known I shall be able to put it to the back of my mind forever.

The cold air whips at my cheeks and lifts the curls from my brow. It is good to be alive and I am suddenly aware of my own selfishness. In a way Betsy was right. For too long I have moped and grieved, whilst all the time being in the possession of those most precious gifts—recovered health, a good husband and a beautiful baby son. I feel wonderfully alive again after so many days of lethargy, and nothing Jake Minns can tell me will take this exuberance away from me. Once I know everything I shall inform my husband—we must be totally honest with each other from now on—and then I shall tell him to forget everything about my past, as I have done, and we will move forward together to a new future.

Smiling into the wind I turn my head and look at my companion. 'I believe you have something to tell me, Mr Minns? Mother Scurry told me to speak to you. What is it you have to say?'

We have slowed to a walk, making for the small copse at the top of the rise. Jake Minns looks back at me with his hot black eyes, and I put out a hand to touch Cloud's silken neck; the warmth of her strong body is reassuring as my composure begins to crumble.

'Well, what do you want to tell me? You stare at me so often your attention disconcerts me.'

'I could not believe that you was the same person, ma'am,' he says at last, his eyes burning into my face. 'I knew that it must be you—but so different in looks—' he pauses, shaking his head, 'I couldn't be sure.'

'Who am I, Mr Minns? At least, who was I

before my marriage? And how did I come to lose my memory?'

' 'Twas a terrible thing,' he answers softly, turning his penetrating gaze upon the trees ahead of us.

His nose is hooked in profile, and with his black beard and locks he resembles a gypsy, or a pirate.

'What was so terrible? Go on, man, tell me!'

'You came from the Old Priory, ma'am, and there was a fire there one night, a great blaze within those bricked-up walls, and very few holy women escaped.'

'A convent!' I stare in astonishment. Not me, who dislikes Parson Andrews, who finds the services boring and the church cramped and musty. Me, a woman of prayer and contemplation? It cannot be.

I smile, but my lips are dry and my hands feel slippery on the reins. 'You must be mistaken,' I say, 'but go on, your tale is quite remarkable.'

'I first sees you stumbling about in a field, about half a mile from the smoking ruins. Your shaven head was bare, your garments torn and singed, and that gash—' he nods soberly at me, 'that gash dripping with blood. It was night, but there was a full moon and you was stumbling and falling, making your way towards the road. Dazed, you was, and half-demented; a strange, wild creature with the face of an angel.'

'Go on,' I whisper. His voice is gruff and he is speaking so intently it is impossible not to believe him.

'A burning timber, I reckon it was, something heavy, making that wound and setting fire to your garments. You was shivering and moaning—like some frightened beast—but you was lucky to get out alive.

'I am in the fields, been poaching, ma'am, and sees the blaze at a distance and goes over to see if I can help. Then I sees you all distressed, like, and I'm coming across to help you when I hears this carriage coming fast along the road. I ducks behind the hedge, not wanting to be caught with the pheasant, you understand, and you stands there in the middle of the road, holding yourself with your arms around your body, turning your head from side to side, half-crazed with fear and pain. And the horses are pulled up sudden, ma'am, and he gets down.'

'He?' My heart is pounding with such force that I have difficulty in breathing.

'Mr Hawton, ma'am. I knows he is from Ladylea, though I wasn't working there at the time. And down he gets and talks to you—I can't hear what he says, but he takes your arm and coaxes, like, and then he lifts you into his carriage before driving off into the woods.'

'Oh, no!' Not Mr Hawton. He would not do a thing like that, not with an innocent girl!

'I follows, ma'am, wondering if I can help.

150

But what can I do against the likes of him? He is well known in the district, he could lose me my job—I dares not risk being seen. So I whispers in the horses' ears, making them bolt, hoping that I've startled him and nothing can have happened to you inside in the darkness.'

Mr Hawton, the man to whom I am married, to act thus? I lean forward over Cloud's neck, burying my face in her rough mane. This is the man to whom I have offered myself as a dutiful wife, with whom I was willing to share my bed. This loathsome creature is my husband—and Charlie's father!

No wonder Mr Hawton has not touched me since; he has hidden me away just as he has tried to hide his guilt. But he had his devilish way with me once, and I gave birth to Charlie. Would that he had never been born!

I lift my head at last and turn to my silent companion, forgetting that I once feared him. 'What shall I do, Jake Minns? Where can I go? It is not possible to remain any longer at Hazelwood.'

'Mother Scurry will help you, ma'am, you must go to her.'

'Yes, she told me to go—she was expecting me and Charlie earlier only I had not heard your tale then and could not understand her agitation.'

Shocking, Mr Hawton had said. Indeed it was shocking; no wonder he had begged me to cease questioning him. And this accounts for his dark moods and frequent trips to London. He is as uncomfortable in my presence as I am in his; every time he sees me he must remember.

My heart lifts as I think of the rubies—I am glad, glad that they have gone. And tonight I shall take the pearls, and every other trinket he has given me; not to keep—foul souvenirs of a wicked man—but to sell. I must be able to look after myself and Charlie until our future is decided. Dear Lord, what will become of me and my little son?

'You are speaking the truth?' I turn upon the groom in a fury of passion. There have been so many lies—how can I know if he speaks the truth?

'I do not lie, lady. Here.' He fumbles in his jacket pocket and produces something which glints in the sun. It is a silver cross and chain and he hands it to me with a nod. 'I found that in the woods near where the carriage stopped. He must have torn it from your neck and flung it away. I found it caught amongst the bushes.'

Gently I slide the chain between my fingers, holding the cross in the palm of my hand. It brings back no memories, but gives me strength and reassurance.

'Thank you, I believe you now. It is a wretched tale but I am grateful for the truth, at last.'

'There's one good thing, ma'am,' he says, as we turn the horses and begin the long ride back.

'What is that?'

'Your memory going like that, ma'am. 'Twas a blessing in disguise, if you take my meaning.'

I nod. Poor innocent girl. I can look upon her from this distance as being nothing to do with me. Half-stunned, as she must have been from her head wound, that violent assault upon her body must have been the final blow which snapped the thread of memory within her mind. But her fate no longer concerns me, it is now that is important; the woman I have become, the life I lead. As the house comes into view I pull Cloud to a halt, a shiver running through me. How can I go in, smile and talk, face him across the dining-table as if I have not a care in the world?

'I cannot do it,' I say through clenched teeth, 'I can't go back.' It is not fear which makes me tremble, for Mr Hawton has done nothing these last two years to make me afraid, indeed, his behaviour *has* been irreproachable. Making amends, as he once told me. Pah! But I tremble with wrath, hating and despising the self-willed brute to whom I am wed.

'You must, ma'am.' Jake moves to my side and I can feel his nearness although we do not touch. 'You must go into the house and act normal tonight. Only a few more hours and then you can escape to Mother Scurry. But you must wait until everyone is asleep, no one must see you go.'

'You will not let him find me? I could not bear it if he made me go back—and I am his wife. How can you hide me, you and Mother Scurry?'

'Let us worry about that.' His eyes are dark and compelling. 'All you have to do is get through the rest of this day and make your escape about midnight. I shall be waiting by the stables and will escort you down the lane to her cottage.'

It is comforting to hear that I need not walk that distance on my own in the dark. 'But what of Charlie?' I say quickly. 'He might awaken and cry out.' He will not understand, poor lamb, and could ruin my plans before I am out of the house.

'I shall fetch something from Mother Scurry—something to make him sleep. You can see that he drinks it?'

I nod. Every evening I go up to the nursery to kiss Charlie goodnight, it will be possible to slip something into his milk without Helen noticing.

'I shall bring a packet to the back door and give it to Mrs Wanstead,' Jake Minns continues, 'and tell her you asked me to purchase something in the village. I'll bring it this afternoon, ma'am, do not fear.'

'I think,' I say slowly, riding on again, 'I think I should like to go to Ladylea, to Annie Malthouse. She has hidden me before and I need a place to rest, a sanctuary where I can find time to think and sort myself out.'

'Annie Malthouse? The old groom's wife? What do you know of her?'

I put a hand to my brow; my head is beginning to ache and I feel bewildered and very tired. 'She hid me. Mr Hawton took me to her cottage after—afterwards, and she kept me hidden away there until I recovered. Why do you suppose he bothered about me, Jake Minns? Why didn't he just leave me out there in the woods?'

'Maybe he was scared you would talk—he wanted to keep an eye on you, like. Always wondered what he done with you in that terrible state you was in. Thought maybe it was London you went.'

'You didn't know? Then how did you know to come here to Hazelwood?'

'I knew nothing until I gets a job at Ladylea and then Helen comes south with the boy. And when I sees her we get talking, and the babe loves the horses so they are often around the stables. She tells me Mr Hawton is married and I puts two and two together, ma'am. I never knew you had a child till then, see. But I reckoned if I stayed at Ladylea long enough I'd find out something, and I felt kind of responsible with you being not yourself and no one to speak for you. Mr Hawton came to visit his mother, and I knew if I watched and waited I'd hear news of you, somehow.'

'Annie Malthouse kept me hidden all those

weeks and nobody knew about me?'

'She and old Ted put it about that they'd a niece staying with them, not right in the head, they said, and no one was allowed in the cottage at that time. I heard rumours, people always talk, but though I had me suspicions I couldn't be sure, and you was gone before I could find a way to catch a glimpse of you.'

'Would you take me there, Jake Minns? Help me on the journey and get me and Charlie safely to Sussex? Mother Scurry is too close, I cannot stay there long for Mr Hawton will be certain to find me.'

I tremble at the thought of him and his rage. Having housed and fed me, showered me with beautiful clothes and costly jewels to ease his conscience, he will not accept my flight with equanimity. And his anger will be all the more terrible now that I know the truth. For if I once speak and tell the world about his profanity, how appalling it will look. Even a man with 'extravagances', as his mother had once so delicately put it, would be scorned by society if they knew of his shocking behaviour towards me.

'Hurry, Jake. Go to Mother Scurry and get something for Charlie as quickly as you can. We must get away from here tonight—I feel as if something dreadful is about to happen.'

Premonition, a feeling of terror, envelops me.

'I must rub down the horses, ma'am, else I'll

have Old George ranting and raving. But the minute I'm free I shall go for you. And keep calm, my lady, in a few short hours all will be well.'

'So easy?' I smile without humour. 'I doubt that it will be as simple as that. Mr Robert Hawton is too used to having his own way, he will be a dangerous opponent. However, I am quite determined on leaving Hazelwood—nothing on earth will make me stay in that hateful house any longer.'

NINE

I make a tremendous effort that evening. Betsy is summoned to dress me and it is to be my rose-pink gown, the one she flung at my feet but a few weeks ago. Now, however, I am in command of the situation and nothing that she, or anyone else, can do or say will affect me.

She comes, a little surprised by my call, though she tries to disguise it. Since my recovery I have managed without her assistance, disliking to have her in my bedchamber, keeping her at a distance whenever possible. But tonight is different. It is the last time I shall ever see her demure, deceitful face, and the thought pleases me. I shall be free! Free of her, free of Adam, free of the beast whom I once called husband, free to start a new life with Charlie—God willing.

'Fetch the curling-tongs, Betsy, I wish for an elaborate hair-style tonight.' This will irritate her, for it will take time which she does not care to spend on me. 'I am celebrating with Mr Hawton this evening. I feel so well and happy—a new life is opening up before me and Hazelwood will never be quite the same again.'

I smile at Betsy's sour expression, feeling my heart begin to pound beneath my tightly laced bodice. I shall act as I have never acted before, show Mr Hawton the sort of wife I could have been; let the knife turn in the wound, let him remember this night all his days. And if there is an ounce of decency in him, let him regret his past action and wish that things might have been different.

Now that the veil of secrecy has been lifted, now that I know the worst, the worry and gnawing anxiety about my past have also lifted, and revenge is sweet. Although the truth is horrible, I feel a strange release and know that I can be attractive, have a new confidence in myself, realise that being a beautiful and charming hostess is not beyond my capabilities. And all the knowledge I lack can be learnt, I have only to study the right books, imitate the right people, and I, too, will be able to take my place in society. It is only that I have been lacking the social graces, and despite Miss Hodges's tuition, have not been able to perform adequately because I had no confidence in myself. But my education was not neglected, hence my knowledge of French and Latin, and I could quickly learn the accomplishments of a high-born lady, given the chance.

I do not think that I can have been an exemplary nun, for I am not the least pious and long for excitement and attention. Or did my foul misadventure change my character? No matter. In the future I am determined to make up for everything, I shall make a new life for myself and Charlie and become so popular that even my mother-in-law will admire me. My mother-in-law? She will no longer be that. Hopefully, Mr Hawton will divorce me, or perhaps I have reason enough to divorce him? A lawyer must be consulted as soon as I am settled somewhere; then, maybe, I shall meet a gentle, loving man who will want to marry me and give me and Charlie a home. Unhappily, a woman on her own is both vulnerable and unacceptable. Yet how can I meet people if I am cowering from the world in Annie Malthouse's cottage?

A sudden idea comes to me as Betsy begins curling my hair. Mrs Hawton. I shall go to her and explain the whole story, and Annie Malthouse must be my witness. Then my mother-in-law must help to launch me into society, under a new name, and thus my new life will begin at Ladylea.

'Be careful, Betsy, I do not want my curls burnt to a cinder.'

She starts at the tone of my voice, then begins winding the hair more gently around the tongs. 'I don't know what's got into you, ma'am, you look like a cat that's got at the canary.'

'Maybe I'm a little tired of being the poor caged canary, and have become the cat, Betsy. 'Twas time I grew up and became the mistress here. Sometimes I have allowed other people to frighten me, and have forgotten the authority I really possess.'

Her little white face stares at me in the mirror and I look coldly back. 'Thank you, that will do. Now arrange the curls as becomingly as you can—no, not that way, foolish girl, round the face. Yes, that is better. And you need not wait up for me, Betsy. I am sure you will enjoy an early night. Are you expecting a visitor? No? Well, never mind, take a book with you instead. Tidy up here, please, and then go to your room. I shall see you in the morning.'

She fastens the pearls around my neck and I can see from her expression that she wishes they were a rope.

'Do not frown, Betsy dear, it ages you so. Aren't these pearls beautiful? I do love jewellery but then so do you, I forgot!' I laugh lightly and reach for the few rings I have left. 'There—those will do. I can see that Mr Hawton will soon have to buy me some more. I'll not be rising early so you can sleep late also. Good-night, Betsy.'

And that means goodbye.

Now for Mr Hawton. He had been away at lunchtime, to my relief, and now I am recovered from my shock and in such an odd state of mind that I do not fear meeting him at all. Indeed, I am looking forward to our final, triumphant meal together.

I sail down the stairs, pink taffeta rustling

around my feet, and join my loathsome husband in the drawing-room.

*   *   *

'What has happened to you, Miranda?' He surveys me from over the rim of his glass, as we sit opposite each other at the dining-room table. 'You are different tonight.' He is half-amused, half-concerned, as I gaze serenely back at him.

'The fresh air has done me a power of good and I feel wonderfully well, sir.'

'You enjoyed your ride and will come with me tomorrow?'

I nod, allowing my mouth to curve in a smile.

Scum! Rat! I lower my eyes hastily lest he should read their expression. Never will I ride with you—nor speak with you again, thank God!

'Perhaps you would also be interested in seeing the new school buildings? Now that you are so much stronger you might like to accompany me when next I go to inspect the construction?'

'I should like that, sir. I have been shut away here for too long and need to widen my interests.'

'And Miss Hodges? She is pleased with you?'

'I am a most attentive pupil and will soon

know exactly how a lady should conduct herself, and order her household.'

'Then we must invite guests here, Miranda, and allow you to display your newly acquired knowledge.'

I look at him. 'Do you not find it strange that I know so little about everyday life? I wonder how I was brought up. Did you know my parents, sir?'

'Not that again, Miranda.' He stirs in his chair and a frown creases his brow. 'I had thought that you were content now and determined on living your new life with confidence. Do not start pestering me again, I beg.'

How uncomfortable it must be for him, forever turning his back on the past, slapping me down like an inquisitive child which must be taught its manners, repressing memories which must arise frequently to torment him.

'I shall never cease wondering,' I retort, 'and all the more so now that my brain is clear and I suffer less often from migraine. It is only natural to be curious about oneself and one's background. I find it most peculiar that you continue to withhold information from me.'

It is foolish to keep goading him, especially when it does not matter any more. But I cannot leave without causing him some annoyance—why should he not be made to suffer?

'I wonder if my mother still weeps for me at night, or has she quite recovered from her loss, do you think?'

'Your mother?' He stares. 'You have no mother.'

'Then I am an orphan?'

Mr Hawton shakes his head irritably. 'I do not know, Miranda. I have told you before that there is a great deal I do not know about you.'

'Then when did we first meet? How were we introduced?'

He stands up abruptly, making the glasses shiver on the table. 'Let us go into the drawing-room and discuss our first dinner-party. Your active brain obviously needs something to occupy it. We will make out a guest list and arrange a date so that you can speak to Mrs Wanstead in the morning.' His voice is controlled but his eyes are angry. 'I can see that you need occupation now, Miranda, and playing at hostess will hopefully keep your mind and your hands busy.'

'You make out the list,' I tell him, sweeping past into the hall. 'You know the people, for I have no friends and cannot assist you. I shall retire early, if you do not mind, I am weary.'

'As you wish.'

He watches me as I ascend the stairs and halfway up the flight I pause and look down at him. 'Pray do not come in to bid me goodnight for I shall be asleep.'

He bows but does not speak and I continue

164

on my way, head held high, triumph in every step.

*   *   *

I wait. At twenty minutes to eleven I hear Mr Hawton come upstairs, and see the light of his candle through the crack in the door which adjoins our rooms. At eleven o'clock the light is snuffed out and ten minutes later I begin to dress myself. My oldest gown, a warm cloak, my stoutest shoes, but these last carried and not to be put on my feet until I am out in the back yard. In a knotted bundle go the pearls and the few gold trinkets and rings which remain in my possession.

I dare not light a candle but fortunately it is a clear moonlit night and, having previously ascertained exactly where the windows are, I tiptoe down the passage, pulling back the curtains as I go. There is light enough to see my way past Betsy's door and on to the further flight of stairs which leads to the nursery rooms above. Thank heavens I need not pass this way again, but can take the back stairs down to the servants' hall and then out through the back door. There is also no likelihood of Bella's hearing me, for she sleeps in the library on the far side of the main entrance hall.

The nursery is in darkness but I know the room well, and have pulled aside the curtains and reached Charlie within seconds. He is sleeping peacefully, no doubt helped by the potion which I was able to pour into his milk whilst Helen was searching for a mythical jacket, which I insisted Charlie should wear in the morning.

'A brown one, with little gold buttons,' I had told her, and the puzzled girl had spent several minutes searching in cupboards and drawers, muttering that she had never seen the garment which I described.

Now I bend over my son and lift him carefully from his warm bed. He does not move as I wrap a blanket around him and settle him in my arms. Then, with child, shoes and bundle firmly grasped, I move out onto the landing and make for the back stairs.

I reach the kitchen without mishap, unlock the back door and am out—hope leaping within me as I hurry across the yard, under the archway to the stables.

Jake Minns moves from the shadows to greet me. 'Give me the babe,' he says quietly, 'we must hurry.'

I hand him Charlie and stoop to put on my shoes before following him down the lane.

It seems an age before we reach Mother Scurry's cottage, and all the while I am terrified lest shouts or pounding footsteps sound behind us and announce that our flight has been discovered. But all is quiet in that eerie, milky stillness save for the occasional hooting of an owl, and the muffled tread of our feet as we walk, Jake Minns leading, across the furthest field to our refuge.

Mother Scurry opens immediately to our knock and I am thankful to sit before the fire and get my breath back, for Jake Minns has moved at a brisk pace.

'At last!' Her voice is rasping but low as she busies herself at the stove. 'A good cup of tea, mistress, and then a lie down on my bed whilst Mr Minns and I make our plans. You must be weary, but now you are safe. Nobody heard you go, eh?' And she peers round at me with her hooky nose and sharp eyes, looking very like an owl herself.

'I do not think so.' I lay my head back against the chair and close my eyes, grateful for the warmth and security of the cramped room. 'Everything went according to plan.'

'Place the child on that cushion beside the bed, I made it ready for him,' Mother Scurry tells my companion, and then hands me a cup of tea. 'Drink that, dearie, and then onto the bed with you. You will need sleep before the morrow.'

Jake Minns is standing by the table and the old woman turns on him. 'Stop your fidgeting, man, and sit yourself down. There's time enough to spare so save your legs—you'll be needing them later.' Then she bends over me and I feel her hand on my hair. 'There, dearie, doesn't that feel better? Now let me help you to bed.'

I rise and lean against her, surprised by my fatigue, but then I am assisted to the bed, a rough blanket is thrown over me, and within seconds the room blacks out and I am asleep.

When I awake the room is deserted and the candle out, the only light coming from the fire in the hearth. My head still feels muzzy and I move to sit up but cannot shift hands or feet. My ankles are bound and my arms, folded across my breast, are tied at the wrists. My eyes are wide open now and I stare upwards in horror, wondering if I am going insane. Who has done this? For what purpose? Where are Jake Minns and Mother Scurry?

In a panic I bend my neck and peer sideways to see if Charlie is still there. To my relief I see the corner of the cushion and one of Charlie's little feet is just in view. But is he alive? Fear overwhelms me, and with a gigantic effort I fling my body upwards and forwards into a sitting position. The action makes my head drum with pain but I can see all of Charlie now and he is asleep, his head turned towards me, and his mouth is blowing imaginary bubbles with every breath.

I fall back onto the hard lumpy bed and try to think. It must be them—the groom and the old woman—who have done this to me. But why try to stop me escaping? I have come to them for aid. Why should I decide to run from them? My heart is pounding beneath my clenched fists and I feel very frightened. Something is badly wrong—have we been left here to die? Nobody knows that Charlie and I are here and we could remain in this hovel, undetected, for days, even weeks.

As I wonder, voices sound faintly from outside and I close my eyes and try to steady my breathing. What will happen now?

'You cannot go yet—you must help me with the girl.' Mother Scurry's voice is sharp and querulous. 'Only till the dawn, Mr Minns, then you may go where you wish and take the brat with you.'

They enter the cottage and somebody moves to my side. 'It will soon be time to waken her.' The old woman's voice rises in excitement. 'This is something I have waited for all these long years, Mr Minns, the ultimate sacrifice. A virgin and child, it says in the book, but how can such a thing be, I've always said. Now here is the answer—and she has fallen for our plans and come as sweetly as a lamb to its slaughter.'

My heart is drumming so loudly that it feels as if it will burst from my chest—can she not hear the thumping? Dear God, what does she intend doing with me? What ultimate sacrifice?

Someone pokes at the fire and a chair creaks.

'She came from the convent,' says Jake Minns. 'I can vouch for that.'

'And that fool of a husband has served me well!'

'I don't like it, Mother, danger is very near. Let us take her out now and be done with it. I must be away from here by daylight.'

'You'll wait until the dawn, Mr Minns, and assist me as you promised. I cannot carry her alone and who knows—the Horned God may look kindly upon you for your work this night.'

Blood pounds in my heart, in my ears, in my brain. I want to scream but dare not make a sound. How can I escape their devilish clutches? The other cottages are too far away and no one would hear my cries for help.

'I do not believe in your gods, Mother.' His voice is rough. 'Have a care, for Mr Hawton is a savage man and you'll not get away with this fiendish act.'

'That is my concern and the Potter girl knows what to say. When I helped rid her of the unborn baby she promised to do what I said. Besides, she is frightened of me, Mr Minns, and will do what she is told. So, the jewels vanish, as does the mistress of Hazelwood with her child, and the groom. Mr Hawton can spend the rest of his life searching for her but he'll not find his wife.'

'You do not like him, our noble master?'

'I hate him.' Her voice is thick with venom. 'He had me gaoled, Mr Minns, shut up with whores and thieves for twelve long months. The others did not trouble me for they were terrified of my evil eye, so I was left alone in my corner of that hell. But I was trapped, Mr Minns, and could not breathe the fresh air, nor walk in the woods, nor touch the dew on the grass. I vowed then that I would repay.'

'Maybe Mr Hawton will not care if his wife leaves him? He cannot feel affection for her if he has not claimed her body since their wedding-day. What a waste.'

The chair creaks again and I hear a heavy tread moving towards me.

'Don't touch her!' shrieks the old woman, and there is a thump and a scuffle. 'You sit there and leave that girl to me. She is mine, Mr Minns. You may have the child but the girl belongs to me.'

'Won't do you no good,' he says sulkily.

'And why are you grumbling? You get the child, the Potter girl gets the jewels, and I get what I want.' Her voice lifts in a weird howl. 'The final blood-letting, Mr Minns. Eko, Eko, Azarak!'

A moan escapes my lips, I cannot listen any longer, and in an instant she is beside me, and Jake Minns peers from over her shoulder.

'So, we are awake now, my hinny? Awake and not too comfortable? Never mind, dearie, it won't be long before you are free. Free as a bird released from all your worry and fear.'

The old witch leans over me, smoothing my hair with her leathery hands, and her breath smells vile in my face. Whimpering, I try to

171

hide beneath the rough blanket.

'Hurry, Mother—'tis time to go. We cannot delay longer.'

'Very well.' The old woman turns away from me and hobbles towards the door. I hear the creak and clatter as it swings back on its hinges and a gush of cold night air sweeps into the room.

I scream, opening my mouth wide, filling my lungs, then scream again. But Jake Minns is beside me, bending over me, and his tough, calloused hand slams down upon my mouth, crushing my lips.

'Shut up!' His eyes glint above me and his teeth show briefly through the hair on his face in a wicked grimace. 'One more sound and I'll have my way with you whether the old crone minds, or not.'

He does not remove his hand but the pressure lessens, and I feel his thumb begin to caress my cheek, softly, sensuously.

I shut my eyes, trying to pray, trying to remember words I have heard so often in church. But my mind is blank and hope is gone. Oh God. Oh God.

'It is almost daybreak.' Mother Scurry comes back into the room and as she advances on me I see a knife in her hand. She bends forward, baring her gums. 'Not for you, dearie, not yet. But your clothing must go and I dare not untie you. Stand away, Mr Minns, and take the blanket—then cover her nakedness when I

172

have done.'

She rips my skirts and my petticoats, pulls them away from my trembling flesh, cuts the laces of my bodice and peels it from me. Roughly I am turned over onto my side, and the remaining layers of fabric are removed. Half-swooning, I hear her mutter of satisfaction, and then the blanket is thrown over me and I am lifted in hard, muscled arms.

'No!' I struggle feebly, unable to loosen the iron-like grip about my body, then I see Jake Minns's bearded face above me and his wet, hairy mouth descends on mine. The heat, the smell, the nearness, of the man is more than my senses can stand and consciousness leaves me.

When I come to I am lying on ice-cold stone, still bound, with the blanket removed and my naked skin exposed to the elements. In the east there is faint light and Mother Scurry stands with her back to me, her arms raised to the approaching sun. Her hat has gone and her long silver hair hangs down her back. Jake Minns has disappeared and we are alone—myself and the witch—with no sound save for the faint whispering of the trees behind us. I am shivering uncontrollably from cold, shock, terror, and my mouth is so dry that my tongue clings to the roof of my mouth.

Charlie? My throat works, trying to call his name, but I cannot make a sound. Then Mother Scurry turns and in her right hand the knife gleams. She is uttering strange, unfamiliar words, a chant of gibberish, and as I look up into her haggard face I see madness in her eyes.

As in a trance I watch the blade, waiting for her hand to fall, and then a sound breaks the silence, a sound so faint, so distant, that she does not mark it and I am not certain if it is imagined, or not. But then it comes again, nearer, and as she steps forward to strike, I lift my head and with a tremendous effort force the word—

'Bella!'

The old woman blinks, hesitating, and I swallow and say again,

'It's Bella, Mr Hawton's dog.'

Mother Scurry turns her head to look over her shoulder and as she does so we both hear the baying.

'Bella!' I yell out, hope giving me strength. 'She will catch you, old hag, and tear you limb from limb! Can you hear her now? She is howling for your blood.'

Mother Scurry clasps the knife to her breast, then gathers her skirts with her other hand and with an awful cry of rage plunges past me into the wood.

'Bella!' I call again, less strongly, as tears begin to slide down my face.

It seems like an age before they find me, stretched upon the stone, trussed and rigid. Then Bella is leaping forward to lick my face, and Mr Hawton is shouting to the men to go on and search for the witch, and at the same time grabbing up the blanket from the ground and throwing it over me to hide my shame.

TEN

I am to be sent to Ladylea in disgrace.

Mr Hawton is angrier than I have ever seen him, but it is cold, controlled anger, and there is none of the sympathy one might have expected considering my terrifying ordeal.

'As you are so anxious to know about Ladylea it will be best if you go there and stay with my mother,' he informs me, as I sit opposite him in the library whither he has summoned me.

It is one week later and I have recovered somewhat in mind and body, and have been allowed downstairs for the first time.

Mr Hawton is seemingly relaxed, with his long legs stretched out before him, sitting in his armchair beside the fire. But his face is expressionless and his eyes are bleak.

'You have acted like a stupid wanton,' he says, 'running about questioning and listening to others, trying to find out the truth against my advice.'

'Naturally I sought information elsewhere,' I burst out, 'because you hid the facts from me!'

'And believed that silly Potter female and her accomplice? Behaving like a whore in your husband's home?' His fists clench on the arm rests of his chair. 'If you needed loving so badly I could have given it to you. What an ignorant fool I was! Believing you to be so frail, so vulnerable. But there—' he smiles without mirth—'I behaved as a gentleman should and was made a cuckold in my own house.'

'I did nothing wrong, sir. If Betsy or Adam told you otherwise, they lie! And you are to blame for all this, for you are the criminal, not I!'

He ignores me. 'And what of the jewels? Did you give all the pieces to Betsy's friend, or is my erstwhile groom also the richer by several hundred pounds?'

'I gave them to Adam—he promised to go down to Ladylea and find out the details of my background. He said he needed payment for his journey and as I had no money I gave him my jewels instead.'

'And bedding with him was further reward?'

I sit forward, feeling the blood hot in my cheeks. 'I never went to bed with Adam Rushmore—he has lied and cheated all the way. I liked him, yes, and trusted him until I discovered him in Betsy's room one evening. He told me that he'd tell you this wicked story if ever I dared to mention what I had seen. But he never went to Sussex, sir, and he sold my jewels for his own profit.'

Mr Hawton averts his head, staring into the fire. 'I know, I have heard the whole miserable tale from them. You may be pleased to hear that I have sent the pair of them packing, and written Parson Rushmore a few home-truths about his beloved son. But their behaviour no longer concerns me, and jewels can be bought and sold. Unfortunately wives are not so easy to exchange.'

'What do you mean?' It is all going wrong, I had intended accusing him but everything has been switched around so that I appear the culprit, the scorned.

'I mean that I no longer want you here, Miranda.' He returns my gaze and I see hatred in his eyes. 'I gave you my name, my home, food and clothing, comfort and security. I did everything possible to make up for my past mistake. Yet you threw it all back in my face and ran off with one of my grooms. Can you imagine how I despise you?'

How dare he speak to me in such a fashion? He, who had abused my body, ravaged my innocence. He had saved my life, it was true, but if it had not been for his action in the first place I would never have sought Mother Scurry's aid, or become involved with Jake Minns.

'The sooner I leave here the happier I shall be,' I say angrily.

'That will suit me very well. I may have had women—it was only natural when my conscience forbade me to touch you. But we were beginning to build a new life together, Miranda, and I thought that you had begun to

178

feel affection for me, that there was hope for us both. Then you did this. Your behaviour is unforgivable.'

'What of Charlie?' I dig my fingernails into the palms of my hands. 'Have you news of him?'

'No, and I doubt that I will. Why the devil did you choose to go to that harridan's cottage?'

'She also said that she would help me. Oh, why did Jake Minns take him away? What reason can he have had?'

Tears begin to slide down my cheeks for I am unable to contain my grief any longer, and Mr Hawton stands up with an exclamation of impatience and walks over to the window.

'Possibly Minns intends using extortion—demanding money for the boy's safe return. I have two men out searching and they will do what they can, but I doubt that their chances are good.' He shrugs, then turns to face me. It is all my fault, I can see accusation clearly in his eyes. 'I did not know that the old witch remained on the estate. A few years back I had her gaoled on suspicion of witchcraft and sorcery, and when she was freed I warned her never to set foot on my land again. But Farmer Hare allowed her to stay in that wretched abode, without my knowledge.' He frowns. 'A girl child disappeared from the village at that time and I strongly suspected that Mother Scurry had something to do with her disappearance. But the parents did not press charges, they were glad to have one less mouth to feed, I imagine, and twelve months was the most I could give her without better evidence.'

I shiver, folding my arms about my body. Charlie, my little son, where are you now?

'Helen Morris will go with you to Ladylea,' Mr Hawton goes on. 'I hope that you have shown due gratitude. If she had not woken that night and seen that Charlie's bed was empty you would not be alive today.'

I nod; I have thanked her, over and over again.

'She came straight down to me and told me what she had discovered, and then we found that you had gone, also. That Potter girl told me her delightful tale of how you deceived me with Adam Rushmore, and then, as if that were not enough, relished telling me that you had run away with my groom. Fortunately for you Bella was able to pick up your scent and find you just in time. We have caught the old hag and she is in the asylum where she belongs. But she'll not live long, she is quite demented.'

I shudder. Hatred and anger are spent and exhaustion has drained me of further speech.

'Tomorrow you go to Ladylea, Miranda, and I have told Mother only that her erstwhile groom has abducted Charlie, and that you are distraught and need to get away from Hazelwood for a time. How long you remain there will depend on many things; at least your absence will allow me breathing-space in which to decide what to do with you.'

*   *   *

Helen is very gentle, very kind and sympathetic—so different to Betsy Potter. Her grief is real and deeply felt and she blames herself for this tragedy.

'It was me who brought Jake Minns up here, ma'am, and I can't never forgive myself. If it hadn't been for me you would not be in distress and Charlie would be with us now.'

She sobs silently, great tears sliding down her cheeks as she moves backwards and forwards across the room, folding away my clothes in readiness for the morning's journey.

I lie on my bed, resting my head back against the pillows. Thank God she does not ask what I was doing at the witch's cottage so late at night.

'Do not worry, Helen, you are no more to blame than I.'

'But I loved him, ma'am, and thought he loved me. But he was only using me to get to Charlie, I see that now. How could he do such a wicked, cruel thing? And what would he be wanting with the little boy?'

I shrug, fighting back tears. That is what we all want to know.

'Did you know that Jake Minns was a

181

whisperer, Helen?'

She stares open-mouthed.

'He could cast a spell over the horses by whispering in their ears, so the old witch said.'

Helen shakes her head in bewilderment. 'I only seen him talking to them, ma'am. He had a way with him, like. But a whisperer? I never heard that name. It's creepy.' And she shivers.

'He was a strange man, but he did like Charlie, didn't he? You don't suppose he would hurt a little boy, do you, Helen?'

'Oh, ma'am, no! He was ever so fond of Charlie, and the babe adored him. He won't harm our Charlie, I'm sure of that, ma'am. There now, don't you cry or you'll set me off again!' She comes and puts an arm around my shoulders and I lean against her breast, exhausted.

'They'll find him, won't they, Helen?'

'It's Daniel and John who've gone searching, good men, both of them. They'll find him if anyone can.'

'Mr Hawton is so angry with me. He thinks Jake Minns will demand payment for Charlie's safe return.' I should not speak about my husband to a servant but I have to tell someone. 'He does not want me here any more and is sending me to his mother and she dislikes me. What will become of me, Helen?'

'There, there, you'll become strong and well again down at Ladylea. It's a lovely place, ma'am, and you need to get away from

Hazelwood and all these bad memories.'

'Memories?' I smile weakly. 'I once thought that they were all I ever wanted. Did you know that I had lost my memory, Helen?'

'No, indeed, ma'am.' She looks quite shocked. 'I was told that you had been ill when the master first took me on, and all the other servants knew that you was poorly and suffered from headaches, but we didn't know nothing else.'

Perhaps it is just as well, for what good will it do if others know my secret? I had wanted to escape to Ladylea; had intended informing Mrs Hawton of her son's devilish deed, but now my grief for Charlie is stronger than any other emotion. And Mr Hawton's aid is of infinite importance if I am ever to see my son again.

Perhaps I can talk to Annie Malthouse? The thought calms me, for I am in need of a kind and understanding listener, and Annie might be the right person to advise me. I have not been lucky in my friendships until now— perhaps the old nurse will prove a trustworthy confidante. She, at least, knows about my past and will not require lengthy and involved explanations.

*   *   *

Ladylea is beautiful, as Helen so rightly said. It is a manor-house, part of it dating from Tudor times, and it nestles beneath the Sussex Downs a short drive from the town of Lewes. There is farmland all around and the house is supplied with plenty of butter, milk and eggs. There is a walled vegetable garden, and a flower garden hedged by yew, and at the back of the house sloping lawns stretch down to a small lake.

I saw Annie Malthouse's cottage briefly as we passed up the drive, and at the earliest possible moment I intend calling on her. The cottage did not bring back any memories, presumably because I had always remained within its walls, or in the garden at the rear of the building.

Ladylea is serenly peaceful, and its low-ceilinged rooms are daintily furnished. There is a feeling of home about the place and it has a kinder atmosphere than the dark, high, heavily furnished rooms at Hazelwood. No wonder that Helen and Charlie were so happy when they came to stay, I could be happy here also, were it not for the burden which I carry in my heart; the aching longing for Charlie, and the dread of what Mr Hawton will decide about my future.

My mother-in-law is shocked to hear about Charlie, but her feelings are all for herself and do not extend to me.

'What a calamity—how did that wretch manage to lay his hands upon the boy?' She looks at me accusingly with her dark eyes. 'He was my only grandson—I do hope that Robert is doing everything possible to get Charles back. Your place should be by his side, Miranda. Despite your grief you should have remained there to comfort and sustain him. A wife should not leave her husband alone under any circumstances.'

Shall I tell her what her son is really like? I think bitterly. But it will do no good, it is Charlie I want now, my little son safe in my arms again.

'I hope to return to Hazelwood soon,' I answer quietly, longing to escape upstairs to the room where Helen is unpacking. But Mrs Hawton insisted upon this interrogation.

'And what will happen when the child is found? With both you and Helen here at Ladylea, who will care for the babe? Charles will need his nursemaid, if not his mother.'

'I am sure Robert will bring him immediately to us, Aunt Edith,' says Miss Somerset, glancing at my face. 'And Miranda can do nothing to help up there with Robert and the men out searching. It is better that she stays quietly here with us.' She smiles at me. 'Try not to worry too much—I am sure everything will turn out all right in the end and Charlie will be found.'

'But why bring the nursemaid?' Mrs Hawton looks down her nose at me. 'She should have remained at Hazelwood. Where is that other person whom you had before, your personal maid?'

'She has gone,' I answer faintly. 'Mr Hawton dismissed her.'

'I suppose she had something to do with this miserable affair? Never trusted her. I could see at once that she was a deceitful minx. Why you young women cannot be better judges of character, I'll never know. Only last week that new Mrs Butler was telling me of the trouble she had had with her servant, and I told her that I would have known the moment I set eyes on the creature. I can always tell when—'

'Your son engaged Betsy Potter, ma'am,' I answer shortly and stand up. 'If you will excuse me, I wish to retire.'

I bow to her and incline my head towards Miss Somerset before turning and walking towards the door.

'Of course, you must be weary after your journey. Allow me to show you to your room.' The younger woman rises and hurries to my side. 'I expect you will find our passages a bit muddling at first—it is rather a topsyturvy house, so much has been added over the centuries, but it is in fact not as large as Hazelwood, and you will soon find your way about with ease.'

She leads the way across the hall and up the carpeted stairs.

This is what we need at Hazelwood, I think. There the wooden staircase rings hollow to one's tread and a carpet would be warmer and softer. And more white paint. Our rooms are dark and gloomy and need brightening. When Charlie comes home, when I go back to greet him, we will celebrate by painting and re-organising the house.

I catch my breath. What point is there in planning? Even if I have my son again I could not bear to live with the man who is my so-called husband. What future is there for the two of us? My head begins to ache as I follow Miss Somerset into the bedroom.

This room is white-painted, also, with a moss-green carpet and curtains, and a gold-flecked bedspread, and a yellow rug beside the bed. There is plenty of cupboard space and the few belongings I have brought with me scarcely fill a quarter of the room provided.

'Do not let Aunt Edith upset you.' Miss Somerset stands near the door, running an observant eye over the room, seeing that all is in order. 'Her bark is truly worse than her bite and she means well. She loved Charlie, too, you know.'

'I know, we all did.' But love alone will not bring my son back.

'I hope you sleep well. Helen has been given a room just down the corridor so she will be close by to attend to your needs. And do stay in bed tomorrow, Miranda, rest all you can, it will do you the power of good.'

'Thank you.'

She leaves me alone then and Helen helps me to undress before bringing me a glass of

187

warm milk.

'The servants are ever so nice, ma'am, and have welcomed me back with open arms.' She looks tired but happy. 'They wanted to know all about that Jake Minns, of course, but I haven't gossiped much. Just told them the bare bones and that you is upset and having a rest down here for a while. I'll bring you up breakfast in bed, ma'am, and you take things easy like Miss Somerset said. I'm right glad we've come, ma'am, and you'll feel a different person in a day or two, you wait and see.'

*   *   *

I have to see Annie Malthouse and talk to her about my pathetic past. But I cannot visit her openly, for what excuse is there for calling on Mr Hawton's old nurse? My mother-in-law will think me odder than ever.

So I take to walking, refusing her offer of a mount from the stables, explaining that my head still aches and such exercise will provoke the migraine further. She understands, or appears to, and so Helen and I go for leisurely strolls together in the mornings, and one day I find reason to stop at the cottage by the main gate.

'You go on home,' I say to Helen, 'I shall not be long, but wish to thank Annie for that letter she sent me and tell her the sad news about Charlie.'

Helen nods and goes on her way up the drive, whilst I take the paved, overgrown path round to the back of the cottage and knock on the stout oak door.

A small, grey-haired woman stands before me, and at once I am transported back in time, remembering that loving, care-worn face, the plump motherly figure. I am enfolded in her arms and feel instant comfort and peace.

'Oh, Annie, I've come home.'

'There, there, dearie.' She is as overcome by her emotions as I am, and turns away, lifting the corner of her pinafore to dab at her cheek. 'Into the parlour with you and sit yourself down, I'll be with you in a thrice.'

Memory returns again as I gaze about me; the clock over the mantel is familiar, with its bold Roman numerals and comforting tick. I remember also the patchwork cushions on the sofa, and there, surely, is the earthenware jug which used to stand beside my bed, filled with country flowers.

Annie Malthouse returns with a glass of her home-made elderberry wine, her face alight with smiles, her pinafore removed, and her hand going up to pat at her hair in its neat bun.

'Dearie me, what a surprise! And so pleasant to see you well—and all your lovely hair grown. A great difference to the last time you sat in this room, ma'am, if I may say so.' She sits herself opposite me, more composed now, beaming with delight. 'I heard tell that the young Mrs Hawton was here a-visiting, and hoped so much that you would drop in to see Ted and me. But I wasn't at all sure if you would remember us.'

'I remember very little, but you are clear in my mind and this room is known to me. For how long did I live here?'

'Four months, ma'am, but so ailing we weren't certain that you would live, poor lady.' She shakes her head and her grey eyes are troubled. 'Mister Robert called whenever he was down and right bothered he was about you, to be sure. But he wouldn't allow me to call a doctor—we kept your secret safely, ma'am, and nobody here knows anything about that dreadful happening. But where is Charlie?' She pats her knees with an impatient movement. 'Here I am chattering away and not thinking to ask about your darling boy. I've heard the news, ma'am, and am right shocked. Have you heard anything more? Have they still not found him?'

I shake my head, misery rising in my breast.

'There, there, now. Mister Robert'll get the boy back—he can do wonders, he can. Don't upset yourself, ma'am, my Mister Robert was always the cleverest of the two, though Mister Simon was his mother's favourite. And he'll work a miracle, just like he did with you.'

'Mr Robert Hawton,' I say through tight lips, 'is the cause of this whole miserable business. I am sorry if you loved him as a child, Annie, but he has grown into a wicked, brutal man and I can never forgive him for what he did to me.'

'Did to you?' She stares, incredulously. 'Why, ma'am, he rescued you, that's what he done. He picked your poor broken body up out of that ditch and brought you here to safety, and gave me money to feed and nurse you all those long weeks.'

'Mr Hawton raped me, Annie.' I am on my feet, standing over her, hatred and fury spilling over in a stream of words. 'He found me wandering about, dazed and wounded from that fire at the convent, and he *knew* I was innocent—my shaven head and garments must have told him that! But, as always, he had to have his way and could not control his desires even when faced with a young girl from the Priory. He assaulted me most brutally, Annie, and because of *him*, your precious Mister Robert, I lost my memory and remain to this day as dim-witted and stupid as *he* made me!'

'My dear lady, sit down. You must not disturb yourself in such a way, and I do beg you to listen to me.' She pushes me gently back on to the sofa, and remains standing, patting my shoulder. 'I don't know who you've been talking to, nor how you came by such lies, but Mister Robert was not the man who wronged you. You must believe me, ma'am. He was the one who saved you—for you were senseless

191

and terribly injured when he found you.'

'That's his story.' I pull away from her caress. 'Of course that is what he would tell you—how could he dare confess the truth.'

'But it *is* the truth, ma'am. Ted was there and saw it all. And my Ted would not lie.'

'Ted?' I stare up at her. 'Your husband was there?' She nods. 'He was driving Mister Robert home after a party over at Lewes that night, and when they saw the glow from the fire they drove further to see if they could help. But the flames had really taken hold by then; terrible to see, Ted said, so they came back here and on the way Ted saw something white lying in the ditch. He calls down to Mister Robert about it and Mister Robert says "Stop the horses, Ted, and let's go and see." And they find you, ma'am, and carry you to the carriage and bring you here.

'Both Ted and me is sworn to secrecy because Mister Robert is so fearful about what the truth will do to you, and he doesn't want the neighbourhood gossiping about your misfortune. So we hide you here, and nobody is any the wiser.

'It is ever such a shock when I realise that you are with child, but Mister Robert has an answer for that, too. "Don't worry yourself, Annie," he tells me, sober like, "I'll marry her and make myself responsible for both her and the child." Ah, he's a good man, is Mister Robert, and he made a great sacrifice in marrying you, ma'am, if you don't mind me saying so. For he was engaged to Miss Somerset and they was all set for a summer wedding.'

'Engaged to Miss Somerset?' I interrupt sharply.

'Yes, ma'am, Miss Somerset.' She is breathing heavily from so much talking, and there are bright spots of colour on her cheeks. 'I'm sorry if all this is a shock—me not knowing what you've been told, but I won't have my Mister Robert maligned by anyone. Though I am right fond of you, ma'am, you must not talk of your husband in such a way. He is a good man, he is.'

I sit stunned. Can it be true? Could Mr Hawton's black moods and odd restraint have been caused only by the fact that he knew me to be a nun, and therefore should never have married me? Was that the reason he dared not touch me? Not guilt, as I had imagined, but respect for my chastity? Was it Jake Minns who had lied?

Mr Hawton had married me, a mindless wretch whom he did not know, and had given up the beautiful Miss Somerset, who would have made him a perfect wife. And I had repaid his charitable act by behaving in a stupid manner, and then accusing *him* of this dastardly crime.

'Jake Minns.' I say the name out loud, my mind darting back to the last time I had seen him; remembering his big calloused hands stroking my face, his coarse lips descending on mine, his hairy face and burning eyes. I had believed him and allowed him to take away my son.

Lowering my head I begin to weep in helpless misery.

'Jake Minns!' Annie echoes my words and there is disgust in her voice. 'So that's who it was! Why did I never think of him before? Always did dislike the man—half-gypsy, he was, skulking around here with his black face and bold eyes. And then he goes up to Hazelwood and runs off with our Charlie— dirty rascal! I hope Mister Robert catches him real soon and gives him the thrashing he deserves.'

I lift my wet face and stare across at her. 'But he is Charlie's father, don't you see? That's why he's taken him. Oh, God! I wish I'd never been born.'

'There, there, you'll think otherwise when the child is safe in your arms again. Now drink your wine, dear lady, and let us talk of pleasanter things. When is Mister Robert coming down to see you? Perhaps he will have good news. You must take heart and not upset yourself further.'

I tell her then the details of my banishment from Hazelwood; my foolish action in trying to run away, the hateful things I said to Mr Hawton, the dreadful knowledge that he no longer wants me as his wife, nor as mistress of his home.

Annie sits very still as I speak, her mouth pursed, her brow furrowed in thought. 'Dearie me,' she says at last, 'what a to-do. Things are a sight worse than what I reckoned. But we won't despair, ma'am.' Her face brightens as she clasps her hands together on her lap. 'I know the very person to help you—a good man, and a wise one. That is, if you are willing to tell him the whole sorry tale.'

'How can anyone help me? I've been such a miserable fool.'

'That's as maybe but we must now try and make amends. I'm thinking of Parson Haleworthy, ma'am.'

I shake my head vigorously. 'Not another clergyman! I have had enough of the parson at home, Annie, and cannot take more sermons and preaching.'

'Meet him just once.' She leans forward earnestly. 'And I think you will change your mind. He used to visit the nuns at the Old Priory, ma'am, and might remember you and know something of your background.'

'Was it not a Roman Catholic order, then?'

'No, ma'am. Protestant ladies, they were, but very strict and what they called an enclosed order. Dreadfully sad, it was, and only three poor creatures alive today—four counting you, out of a community of fifty.'

'Very well, Annie,' I say wearily, 'I do not

195

know how your parson can help me, and if I were once devout then religion means nothing to me any more. I do not want him to pester me, or tell me to go to church more often, but I am in desperate need of sound advice. He could not say that my marriage was invalid, could he?' I stare at my companion in sudden fright. 'He would not make me go back into a convent?'

'No, dearie, no, Parson Haleworthy is a kind and understanding man. He won't make you change now, why, you're a married lady, ma'am, and no one can alter that.' And she nods defiantly.

*   *   *

Annie was right. Her Parson Haleworthy is much nicer than Parson Andrews, in fact I like him very much. Mrs Hawton approves of him, too, which is fortunate, and does not mind that I spend time in his company. He is a grey-haired, thin-faced man, with handsome features and a calm expression. Perhaps he is a little too serious, but when he smiles his face lights up in a most pleasing way.

Soon after our first meeting he drove me over to the place where the Old Priory once stood, and was able to fill in part of my lost past.

'You came here at an early age, about twelve years old, I believe, and were educated by the sisters. I was not in this parish then, but I remember Sister Clare telling me about you.'

We sat in his dog-cart, staring at the blackened remains of a once large establishment. No attempt had been made to rebuild it and Nature was already beginning to claim the broken pillars and rotting timbers; ivy twined itself around the charred bricks, weeds had sprung up amongst the rubble, and the woods all around seemed to be moving in, ready to take over the moment we turned our backs.

I shivered. 'What a desolate place. Were the nuns happy here?'

The clergyman sighed. 'It always seemed an unnatural life to me—all those women, shutting themselves away from the world. If they had worked with the sick, or with children, it would have been laudable. But the sisters belonged to an enclosed order and never stepped out from behind those walls once they entered here.'

'I cannot think that I enjoyed such an existence—what possessed me to become a nun?'

'Your father sent you here,' replied my companion quietly. 'Apparently he was a farmer, who prayed for a son. He and his wife had three, maybe four daughters, and he needed a son to help him on the land, and, I suppose, to whom he could leave his house and fields when he passed on. Anyway, he was a deeply religious man, but not of my parish, I'm sorry to say, for I should have done my best to talk him out of his reckless act. He made a vow that if his wife gave birth to a healthy boy, he would give his eldest daughter to the church.'

'And that was me?'

'You, Sister Louise, as I knew you. And, against your will, I fear, you came here when the son and heir was born.'

'What a cruel thing to do! Does he still live, the man who was my father?'

'That I do not know. I was never told your family's name, nor from whence you came. But I knew you, amongst so many, because of your youth, and for your lovely singing voice.'

'My voice?' I stared at him in wonder. 'I did not know that I could sing.'

'Indeed.' He nodded gravely. 'It was the thing I remembered best about you, and why I particularly mourned when we thought that you had perished. Your voice was so pure and vibrant—it reminded me of a caged bird singing its heart out. I am so very glad that you escaped, my dear.'

'And the others? What happened to the few that still live?'

'They have been taken into another House, but one is blinded and another cannot walk. You would not want to make contact again, would you?'

'No,' I said quickly, 'I am a different person

now and that—that Sister Louise is someone else. No one can make me go back, can they?'

The parson shook his head. 'Too much has happened since that catastrophe, my dear, and the young girl whom the nuns took in and educated is dead. You are Mrs Robert Hawton now, and as such must look to the future, not the past. Annie Malthouse has told me a little of your story, Miranda, now let us leave this sad place and you can tell me the rest of your tale on our way home.'

*　　　*　　　*

Parson Haleworthy has given me hope, and a reason for living. He cannot console me over Charlie's disappearance, all he offers in that direction are prayers, but since my loss of memory, God has become a very distant figure.

'Never mind,' Parson tells me serenely, when I admit my true feelings, 'I shall pray for you and your son and husband, and you shall sing. God understands everything, Miranda, and will look kindly upon you, I have no doubt, despite your lack of faith.'

Instead of preaching at me, as Parson Andrews would surely have done, he is giving me singing lessons, and impresses on me the fact that I possess a gift, and that it should be used.

'Your mother-in-law has a birthday soon, if I

am not mistaken, and as a celebration you will perform for her and her guests, and Miss Somerset will accompany you on the pianoforte. Forget about Mr Hawton for the present, my child, and concentrate on yourself. I think it is time you became someone again, someone of reasonable importance and talent. Now you are the young Mrs Hawton, here on holiday, and you have a beautiful voice. Think only about that and give your audience a superb performance.'

'Before an audience? I cannot do that!' The thought of standing up and singing in front of strangers is daunting. 'I can never behave in such forward fashion.'

'Indeed you can, and you shall. You are going to astound Mrs Hawton and her visitors, and everyone will be so impressed they will be demanding your presence at all their dinner-parties, and you will receive more invitations than can be properly handled.' He smiles his gentle smile. 'You are a young and comely female, Miranda, and 'tis time you had some enjoyment in life. You were imprisoned at the Priory, and were in a similar position at Hazel-wood. Now make the most of your freedom and learn to live.'

He is quite determined and very sure of himself, and me. I find myself following his enthusiastic directions in a bemused state of compliance. But I do enjoy singing. Why did I not realise it before? Presumably I had seldom been in a cheerful enough mood to want to sing; and in church I had kept my voice low for fear of drawing attention to myself. Now, however, I can allow words to spring from my lips without hindrance, and I practise daily with Miss Somerset in the music-room at Ladylea.

Miss Somerset is proving a good and loyal friend, taking a genuine interest in my performance, and never complaining when I keep her over-long at the pianoforte. Her behaviour is all the more remarkable now that I know that she was Mr Hawton's intended bride.

'Did you love Mr Hawton?' I ask, unable to resist asking the question once I know her better.

'Yes.' She looks straight at me and I see sadness and resignation in her blue eyes. 'But once he met you there was no hope for me.'

'When he met me?' I query cautiously.

'There is some mystery about you, Miranda, is there not? I won't question you—but maybe, one day, you will tell me about your past.' She hesitates. 'Robert was often down here, it must have been that winter, two years ago, but he was remote and left us alone, going out frequently I know not where. But I believe he was visiting you at the time, so you must be from this neighbourhood although nobody appears to know you. Anyway, I ceased to exist in his life from then on and accepted that fact

201

long ago.'

'I am sorry.'

She shrugs. 'Clive Wheeler has asked for my hand, and no doubt I shall marry him in time. He will make a considerate husband, I think, but you are fortunate, Miranda, there are not many men like Robert.'

'No.' I turn from her and lift a sheet of music in my hand. 'You must have disliked me very much.'

'Only at first. But once I met you and saw your poor scarred face, I felt pity for you and was glad that Robert had wed you.'

'Because I was unlikely to find another husband with such a blemish?'

She blushes. 'I thought that at first, yes. But the scar has faded quickly, has it not? And I like you very much now and admire the way in which you stand up to Aunt Edith. She is only a dragon on the outside, you know, and has a heart of gold really. I believe she is growing fond of you, also.'

'Nonsense. She will never be reconciled to our marriage and knows quite well that you would have made her son a far better wife. But let us forget about that and run through this piece, if you please.'

Miss Somerset sighs. 'I wish you would confide in me, Miranda. I sense that all is not well between you and Robert. Can you not tell me about it?'

'No. Parson Haleworthy has told me to put

all my worries behind me and this I am trying to do. I am here on holiday and refuse to dwell upon my problems, so do not mention Charlie's name, I beg!'

'I won't, dear.' She ducks her head and plunges into the opening bars of 'Country Lass'.

I sing country songs, pretty, lilting melodies with charming words, for Parson Haleworthy is a collector of such ditties and has many notebooks filled with words and musical notes, which he has written down as he moves around the countryside.

'The Box Upon Her Head' is a thrilling ballad about a serving-maid who is returning home after serving her master for seven years. She meets robbers, and a nobleman, on her way, and manages to shoot three of the robbers but the nobleman only shoots one. I like that bit.

'Pleasant Month Of May' is the parson's favourite, but mine is 'The Country Lass', and I have chosen to end my performance with this song. Miss Somerset has suggested that I dress up in milking-maid's attire, and carry a yoke and two wooden pails on my shoulders. It is fun planning and preparing for the birthday celebration, and Mrs Hawton knows nothing, for she is not allowed near the music-room when we practise, and Helen keeps guard outside in the corridor.

Miss Somerset—Cynthia—is a good friend,

Helen is a respectful and loving servant, and Annie is always waiting for me down at her cottage to offer affection and companionship. My life has suddenly become busy and interesting, and all would be perfect if only I had my son with me. And my husband.

Parson Haleworthy has told me not to think about Robert; to put him and thoughts of Hazelwood to the back of my mind. But sometimes, late at night when I cannot sleep, I lie and remember.

I wish most desperately that I had believed my husband, that our friendship might have developed into love, that I had not sought out Mother Scurry, nor had words with that fiend, Jake Minns. For I was beginning to love Mr Hawton, he was right in assuming that my affection was growing, and then I stupidly threw it all away and wrecked every chance of a happy marriage.

Even kissing and cuddling does not seem repulsive to me now, not if it were with Robert Hawton. And I remember his kindness; the way he gave me the horse I wanted, the clothes and jewels which any other female would have taken with gratitude and awe. Yet I accepted everything he gave me and was still not satisfied.

I wanted the truth, and believed all those wicked lies about my husband without stopping to think that they might not be true. I believed sly Jake Minns, as I had believed

Betsy and her deceitful Adam, rather than trusting in my good and considerate husband. And to think that he had wed me, a girl he did not know, in order to save me from the disgrace of producing a bastard child!

I lie in bed tormenting myself with wretched memories, my arms aching for Charlie and my heart longing for Mr Hawton. But morning comes, thank heavens, and with it a new and busy day, and I am able to throw myself into activity and forget my problems until the next night. And the next . . .

The day has come, the seventh of June, Mrs Hawton's birthday.

My dress is lovely; it is all soft pinks and blues, with white petticoats and a little ruched bodice of white silk with puffed sleeves. No milkmaid was ever attired so richly, but the effect is good. A yoke and two wooden pails have been borrowed from the dairy, well scrubbed and looking as good as new, and I feel more confident thus clad.

The rehearsal has gone well, performed in the morning in front of the servants and Annie Malthouse, and Parson Haleworthy is pleased and promises to be there, giving support, in the evening.

That night, when all the guests are seated, Cynthia settles herself at the pianoforte, which has been brought into the drawing-room, and then I come in through the glass doors behind her, having been waiting in the garden until the final moment.

There is a gasp, then applause, as I stand in my sumptuous costume at the far end of the room. Slowly I set aside my yoke and pails, then move to stand beside Cynthia as she plays the opening bars of music.

Mrs Hawton is seated right in front of the assembled guests, very handsome in pale cream-coloured satin, with a topaz necklace, and long drop earrings of matching gems. I see the Wheelers, and Clive sitting between his parents, his eyes fixed upon Cynthia. The Butlers are there, and the Latimers, and many other wealthy neighbouring families; but I cannot see Parson Haleworthy and my heart sinks. He promised me that he would be present, and I need his encouragement.

Then, as I begin the first verse of 'The Box Upon Her Head', stumbling slightly, my voice weak and uncertain, the door from the hall opens quietly and two figures enter and sit down at the back of the room. But not before I have seen that one is the clergyman and the other is Mr Hawton. They are both smiling, and Parson Haleworthy nods at me and lifts his hand, and I am suddenly confident and ridiculously happy.

Charlie has been found! I know it at once, and the thought lifts my heart and my voice throbs with joy. Sound pours from my throat and I sing as I have never sung those simple melodies before.

There are numerous encores before I finally end my recital, and people rise and crowd around me, congratulating, laughing, exclaiming. Parson Haleworthy was right—there are invitations to sing for this occasion, and for that; my mother-in-law is asked to take me to the Butlers, and will we please dine at the earliest moment with the Latimers? I must entertain all their friends and relations, and widen my repertoire. Do I know this song? Have I tried that one? It is many minutes before I can work my way down the length of the room and greet my husband.

'I am so glad to see you,' I say, my eyes on his face, my hands reaching out for his, 'where is Charlie? Have you brought him with you?'

'Oh, my dear,' answers Mr Hawton softly, holding my hands tightly against his chest, 'I am so sorry to disappoint you—I did not think—Charlie has not been found.'

* * *

Later that evening, as soon as it is polite to do so, I excuse myself and seek the quiet of my room upstairs. But when I open the door it is to find that all my clothes and belongings have gone, the bed is still covered, no fire has been lit, and the curtains are parted, letting in the cold white moonlight. Shocked out of my misery I stare about me, then turn, about to summon Helen, when I see her hurrying down the passage to meet me.

'Oh, ma'am, I have moved everything now, and you and Mr Hawton are to have the Blue Room. I'll just go down for hot water and then you can have a nice soak. You must be quite exhausted. What a lovely evening, ma'am! I peeked in at the window and saw it all. You was a grand success.'

I smile wanly, then allow her to lead me along to the large bedchamber which I am to share with my husband.

Mr Hawton allows me time to disrobe and wash before he comes upstairs, and it is only as I am sitting at the dressing-table, in my night attire, brushing my hair, that he makes an appearance. There is a light tap on the door and Helen opens to him, before wishing us both good night and disappearing to her own room.

'What can I say?' He stands with his back to the door, tall and handsome as ever, but there seem to be new lines around his stern mouth, and he does not look as if he has slept well for a long time. 'Parson Haleworthy wrote to me, explaining the misunderstanding between us, Miranda, and asked me to come down for my mother's birthday. I expect he also wanted me to see what a very accomplished wife I have. You were, indeed, magnificent.'

I remain silent.

'We have done everything we can to try and find Minns and the boy—you must believe that—but they have vanished without trace.' He sighs and moves forward to slump down in the chair beside the fireplace. 'I should have written but did not know how to find the words. I am sorry.'

I place the brush carefully back on to the glass dresser top.

'Was that the only reason you came? For your mother's birthday?'

'No.' He lifts his head and looks across at me. 'The house was lonely and so damned empty—I missed you, Miranda, and wanted to ask if you would come back to me. I know it will be difficult, difficult for us both to forget the things that happened, the words that were said. But if you are willing to try again I shall do my very best to aid you.'

Hazelwood without Charlie. And memories of Betsy and Adam, Mother Scurry and Jake Minns. I shiver and pull my wrapper around my shoulders. Yet if I give up this chance, what future will there be for me? I cannot live on Mrs Hawton's charity forever, and Robert Hawton is a good and generous man. And I love him.

'What of those women in London?' I say, leaning forward to examine my face in the mirror, pretending a nonchalance I do not feel.

'They were nothing to me—I have not been to town since you left. I have been very lonely without you, Miranda, can you believe that?'

'And you will not go again—without me?'

He shakes his head. 'I intend settling down and becoming a good squire and master of my house. And it would make my life easier and infinitely happier if you would share it with me.'

I hesitate. 'What I cannot understand, even now, is why you kept saying that you should not have married me. Why you spoke about your past mistake, and asked me to forgive you. Can you wonder that I believed all that Jake Minns told me—*you* had planted suspicion in my mind to begin with!'

'But don't you see.' Mr Hawton comes swiftly across the room to stand beside me, urgency in his voice. 'I knew that you were from the Old Priory, and should have made arrangements for you to return to a convent somewhere; should have taken Parson Haleworthy into my confidence and asked his advice about your future. Even with a child, under those circumstances appropriate arrangements could have been made for you both.'

'And why didn't you?'

Mr Hawton bends forward and takes my hands in his. 'Because I wanted you, Miranda; wanted you in my arms and in my life. Despite your poor marred face and empty mind I fell in love with you—perhaps because you were so innocent, so vulnerable, unlike any other female I had encountered.

'Yet what a dilemma to be in! Once you were my wife I longed to make love to you, but my conscience forbade it until I had told you about your past.' He lifts one of my hands and holds it against his cheek. 'And that, my dear one, was the problem. For if I spoke about the former tragedy, would it not have affected you mentally? Shattered the confidence in yourself which I was trying so hard to build? You might even have desired to return to a convent. So I played the coward, taking no risks, and kept you imprisoned at Hazelwood. There was also the knowledge that I had behaved immorally, for you were a bride of Christ, promised to God, and I had no right to you.' He sighs. 'Forgive me, Miranda, I acted unwisely but 'twas well meant.'

'What about Cynthia?'

'You have heard about our betrothal?' He shrugs, and lets go of my hand. 'That was to please my mother more than anything. Cynthia is a charming girl and I was fond of her, and Mother felt it was time I settled down. But once I saw you I was determined to have my own way and make you my wife. It was this guilt, my dear, which preyed most terribly on my mind, and when you became stronger and began questioning me about your past, I could scarce bear it. For what could I tell you? How explain my selfish action?'

'Not selfish, sir! You gave me and my son a home and saved us from disgrace.'

He looks down at me and his eyes are full of love. 'You do not regret what happened, Miranda? You can forgive me for hiding you away and concealing the truth? I tried so hard to make it up to you in other ways.'

'I was the selfish one—accepting so much from you and never showing gratitude, or affection—'

'Save once.' He interrupts me, smiling. 'You offered yourself to me so sweetly late one night in the library, and I was fool enough to refuse you. Dear heavens, if I had but taken you in my arms then, we would not have had all this misery to bear.'

'And we would not have lost Charlie,' I whisper. 'Will we ever find him, do you think?'

'I know not, but we'll never cease looking.' Mr Hawton leans forward and draws me to my feet. 'What is your answer, Miranda? Will you come back with me to Hazelwood, to live as man and wife, to begin a new life together?'

'Yes,' I answer, without hesitation.

Then my husband lowers his head and kisses me on the lips for the first time since we were married. It is a most pleasing experience.

EPILOGUE

Mr Hawton and I have five children of our own now; beautiful and intelligent, they fill these big rooms with noise and laughter and Hazelwood has come alive, at last.

Mark is to go to Eton, and little John will follow him when the time comes. My husband is amused by my interest in their education, but I will not have Mrs Cavendish looking down her nose at me again. Margaret, Fanny and Emma have a governess who teaches them needlework and the pianoforte, but they also learn French, Mathematics and English. My daughters are going to be well-schooled also, on that I am determined.

Cynthia and her husband, Clive Wheeler, visit us every year, and I think and hope that she is happy. They have a little daughter now whom they both adore.

Mrs Hawton comes to stay every summer and she likes me somewhat better, for I have done my duty and presented her with enough grand-children to satisfy her. And we go down to Sussex every winter and spend a few weeks at Ladylea during the festive season.

Mother Scurry's cottage has been pulled down, thank goodness, so that the children and I can roam the fields and woods without fear, and the other dwellings on the estate have been improved.

At first Mr Hawton insisted that the cottages were none of his business, that Mr Cross and the tenant farmers would take it amiss if he interfered with their management. But Robert finds it hard to deny me anything, and eventually he came to a decision. He discussed the problem with his steward, and it was arranged that he would accept lower rents from the various tenant farmers for a period of one year, and they, in turn, would use the extra money on improving their labourers' living conditions. This has been done, and I hope that the farm workers live happier and healthier lives. I do not call on them and their families, nor pry into matters which no longer concern me. I learnt my lesson with Betsy Potter and seek only to be a good wife and mother.

Last year when we were down in Sussex, Robert drove us over to Lewes, to the horse fair, for he was looking for a pony for Fanny. In all the hustle and bustle I was separated from my husband and the three older children, little John having been left behind with Helen, and Emma and I were on our own for a while, surrounded by the shouting, jostling crowd.

As I searched around, looking for Robert's tall figure, I spied a boy, who was sitting high upon the wooden railings which penned in a small herd of shaggy-coated wild ponies. He was a black-haired lad, of about twelve years, and something about the turn of his head, the shape of his mouth, caught at my attention.

Pulling at Emma's hand, I pushed my way through the throng until I stood directly beneath him. He turned at my approach and his hand went up to his forehead.

'Good-day, ma'am.'

He returned my gaze with clear grey eyes, and his skin had a warm, out-of-door glow about it.

'What is your name?' I whispered, unable to speak properly, my heart thudding in my breast.

'Jet, ma'am.' He grinned. 'On account of me hair.' And he lifted a hand to touch his thick, unruly mop.

'And your other name?'

'Blake, ma'am.' He looked away, his attention on the ponies, and I caught at his threadbare sleeve.

'Are your family here?' He would have changed his name, of course, yet how could I be certain? Was it just a woman's silly whim, or was there some call of the blood which made me insist on questioning him? 'Are your father and mother with you?'

The boy swung round to look at me again and there was a puzzled expression in his light eyes. 'I ain't got no ma, and me father's some place over yonder.' And he gestured behind him at the crowd.

'Come, Mama, what are we waiting for?'

cried Emma, impatiently. 'Don't keep talking to that dirty boy, I want to go home.'

'In a moment.'

I looked beyond the lad, my eyes seeking a black-haired man with a beard. Then I shivered and turned my attention to Emma, who was struggling to lead me away. I did not want to see Jake Minns again—what use was it now? And it might not be Charlie; there must be many dark-haired boys of that age who were motherless.

'I'm coming now, Emma, let us go and find Papa.'

For a last moment I looked back over my shoulder, and I saw the boy bending forward, catching at the mane of one of the ponies, and as I watched, he leaned forward, smiling, and I saw him whispering into the animal's quivering ear.

'Mama!' Emma wailed. 'Come on!'

Blinking back tears I followed her small figure, and through a gap in the crowd I saw my family sitting in the carriage, waiting for me.

We hope you have enjoyed this Large Print book. Other Chivers Press or Thorndike Press Large Print books are available at your library or directly from the publishers.

For more information about current and forthcoming titles, please call or write, without obligation, to:

Chivers Large Print
published by BBC Audiobooks Ltd
St James House, The Square
Lower Bristol Road
Bath BA2 3BH
UK
email: bbcaudiobooks@bbc.co.uk
www.bbcaudiobooks.co.uk

OR

Thorndike Press
295 Kennedy Memorial Drive
Waterville
Maine 04901
USA
www.gale.com/thorndike
www.gale.com/wheeler

All our Large Print titles are designed for easy reading, and all our books are made to last.